CIRCLE CITY CRIME

Circle City Crime
Presented by:
In Mysterious Company

Edited by Diana Catt
First edition: October 2019

This is a work of fiction. All the characters, places, and events portrayed in these short stories are either fictitious or are used fictitiously.

Cover by: Candice Cooper Design

Cover photo: Soldiers' and Sailors' Monument, Indianapolis, Indiana, by alexeatswhales (IMG_3845) [CC BY 2.0] via Wikimedia Commons

ISBN: 978-0-9963092-2-6

Published by SPEED CITY PRESS
Also available from SPEED CITY PRESS
Decades of Dirt (2015)

CIRCLE CITY CRIME

DEDICATED TO THE MEMORY OF
SUZANNE (S. M.) HARDING

S. M. Harding has had more than thirty short stories published in various markets, both online magazines and in print anthologies and magazines. Two of the most recent include "A Winter Story" in *Wicked Things* and "Spirit of Christmas Past, Christmas Future" in *Unwrap These Presents*, both from Ylva Publishing. Her debut novel, *I Will Meet You There*, was published by Bella Books in 2015 followed by *A Woman of Strong Purpose*, *Speak in Winter Code*, and *A Matter of Security*. She taught classes at the Indiana Writers Center and participated in panels for their annual Gathering of Writers, as well as at Indy Author's Fair, Magna cum Murder and various local libraries. She contributed to and edited *Writing Murder*, a collection of essays by Midwestern authors about writing crime fiction.

You can find Suzanne's website at **www.smharding.webs.com**, her blog at **www.storytellersfire.wordpress.com** and her author's page at **Facebook.com/pages/S-M-Harding**. Suzanne passed away on March 27, 2018.

Suzanne was one of the founding members of the central Indiana writers' critique group which came to be known as *In Mysterious Company*. She wrote under the pen name S.M. Harding. It was her hope that the members of *In Mysterious Company* would put out an anthology of crime fiction based in Indianapolis. She even came up with the title. *Circle City Crime* is our way of honoring her memory.

CONTENTS

FOREWORD
By Sharon Short

What a delight to read this collection of short stories, all of which give a nod to the writers' beloved mentor and teacher, Suzanne Harding (S.M. Harding). The stories range in tone and voice, from laugh-out-loud funny, to thought-provoking, to darkly intriguing. Yet each reflect, either directly or indirectly, Suzanne's spirit and passionate dedication to writing and the writing life: tough, unrelenting and yet ultimately loving in pushing herself, and others, to get to the truth of the piece of writing in question—and to the truth of what the writer wants and needs to convey to readers.

I first met Suzanne in (and I'm guessing a bit here on the year, relying on memory) 1995 (or 1996?) at the Antioch Writers' Workshop in Yellow Springs, Ohio, when I led an afternoon session on mystery writing. While my memory may not reliably serve up the exact year, it does serve up indelible recollections of Suzanne. She gave honest and tough, yet constructive, critiques to her fellow students in the session. Making those critiques even more valid was her ability to not only accept, but eagerly take in and thoughtfully consider, the critiques of her own work. She was steady, committed, and passionate about making her own work better, and honestly passionate about doing what she could to help other writers improve their craft. Though she got to the point—I am sure that Suzanne was not one to suffer fools gladly in her life—her point was always so spot on and delivered with a sincere desire to help (which is quite different than a sincere desire to please, which is rarely, if ever, helpful for writers) that the recipients received her comments with respect. Eventually, that respect would turn to gratitude as Suzanne's comments hit the mark.

Suzanne was, in this way, one of the most grace-filled students I've ever had in a workshop. I'm not sure she'd like that word, as applied to her, but I think it fits. She offered feedback from a deep well within her, from careful and long consideration, but with no presumption that they would be accepted, what's more applied, to the work at hand. And she took in feedback on her work in the same way—with a depth of contemplation and gratitude (even if, after long consideration, she might opt to not apply the feedback) that is rare among writers.

I always had the sense that Suzanne grew from every experience.

I know that I became a better writer, teacher and person from the few times I spent with her. After having her as a student, I was a guest speaker once for the writers' group at Jim Huang's bookstore, and saw her there. She came back another time to the Antioch Writers' Workshop. I followed her career via the internet and social media.

I was not in the least surprised that Suzanne went on to publish many short stories, and then her debut novel, "I Will Meet You There," in 2015.

By then, I was the director of the Antioch Writers' Workshop, which included in the morning sessions of its annual summer program a "First Book Talk" given by an past attendee of the workshop who went on to have published a novel, story collection, poetry collection, or nonfiction book with a traditional, literary or university press. I was so delighted to attend a meeting of the faculty selection committee and say— "we must invite Suzanne Harding to speak at our summer program in 2016!"

We did, and thankfully, Suzanne accepted. Though it had been a long time since we'd seen each other in person, I knew Suzanne—with her distinctive voice and personality—immediately.

Her "First Book Talk" was classic Suzanne. The hard-hitting truths about the challenges of the writing life, learning writing craft, and publishing—but delivered up with a bluntness and, yes, grace, that brooked no rancor or bitterness. This was Suzanne, sharing with us her truth, and the truth of what it means to dig deeply to be a writer, to be in service and devotion to the writing life, in a way that touched every audience member, reminded us to keep our passion for writing as the touchstone of our lives. Every audience member—including me. I'd say "student had become teacher," but I can just hear Suzanne admonishing me not to give in to clichés, and I'd have to aver she was correct.

So instead I'll conclude by stating that it was an honor and joy to read these stories, clearly from the writers' hearts and voices, and yet also an homage to Suzanne's passion and humor and style and voice. Her toughness and grace. Her love of writers and writing and the writing life.

Thank you, Suzanne, for touching so many writers' and readers' lives, and thank you In Mysterious Company for this worthy collection of stories inspired by Suzanne's spirit and guidance.

September 28, 2019

Sharon Short (a.k.a., Jess Montgomery)

FOREWORD
By Jeanne M. Dams

I never knew Suzanne Harding as well as the writers of these splendid short stories. Like them, I first met her at Jim Huang's wonderful and much-lamented mystery bookstore in Carmel, The Mystery Company. We ran into each other at Magna cum Murder, and enjoyed each other's company, and I was very much flattered when she asked me to contribute an essay to her guide to mystery writing, *Writing Murder*.

But I live in far northern Indiana, so I never had a chance to attend her classes or participate in her writing group, and I realize, reading *Circle City Crime*, how much I missed. Working in a group of like-minded writers, with a mentor who knows what she's doing, is a gift beyond price. The stories here, and the heartfelt tributes to Suzanne, bear witness to how very much they know they owe to her. Different stories, different styles, different voices—but all skillful and sure.

Suzanne is surely proud.

Jeanne M. Dams
Author of the Dorothy Martin Mysteries

THE CIRCLE EFFECT
DIANA CATT

My father's admiration for art influenced my life to no small extent. Just so, his fervor plunged me into an ethical dilemma as a young man that I wrestle with to this day. The tale of the events that transpired is both terrifying and regrettable.

The affair began over twenty years ago, in 1887. Indiana's legislation handily approved the money for the greatest monument in the state. and the task to hire the architect proceeded at a fever pitch. The good citizens of Indianapolis were eager to witness a noteworthy use of our city's central circle of land and loyally followed each step in the proceedings of the Monument Commission's contest for designs. Cheers arose from the crowd when they unveiled Bruno Schmitz's winning model.

As a mere child, my father took me periodically to the circle, now commonly called 'Monument Circle,' to follow the progress.

"There will be amazing fountains continually filling clear pools on each side," my father explained as we marveled near the edge of the thirty-foot hole dug for the foundation.

My young mind couldn't begin to imagine the engineering involved in such a project, but I could anticipate the effect.

Over the next ten years the shaft slowly expanded, stage by stage, until the Indiana State Soldiers and Sailors Monument reached its glory of 246 feet. I simultaneously grew in height and maturity during this time. I'd reached my fifteenth year when Schmitz prepared his supporters for the arrival of his artist, sculptor Rudolf Schwarz, who would adorn the monument with intricate groupings reflecting moments of war and peace. My father and his friends found it amusing to provide the philanthropic support to enable Schmitz's vision to become reality. They recognized the sculptor would need a studio near the construction site and were successful in procuring a suitable lot. Because of my father's influence and my able-bodied enthusiasm, I was allowed to assist in modifying the artist's studio to meet his specifications.

We finished preparations for the studio by early December, but we weren't prepared for the man, Rudolf Schwarz. His bohemian appearance and lifestyle fascinated me, and I volunteered to serve in any capacity, just to experience this oddity firsthand. He scrutinized my face and physique while listening to my offer to work before and after school and on my days off.

"Ach, you are the perfect model," he said. "I pay you if I have money, no?"

I laughed at his cavalier attitude. I knew the money came from my father and his friends, but Schwarz didn't seem to concern himself with that level of detail. From the first day, he concentrated on the sculpture and paid no heed to the condition of his workshop, his appearance, or his diet. As long as he had clay to model, stone to carve, and enough money for liquor at the end of the day, he remained in good spirits.

My own aspirations were to study architecture, and I anticipated the chance to examine sketches, plans, diagrams. But, no. This enigma went directly from mental image to clay model. Schwarz worked with amazing concentration and speed, ignorant of the detrital trail he left behind. Each evening before I left, I picked through the litter—metal scraps or wires, lumps of discarded clay, broken plaster casts and other rubbish—in order to locate, clean, and organize his tools. He didn't seem to notice. In fact, he frequently appeared in the morning wearing the same clay-smeared clothes from the previous day, often with gypsum particles still imbedded in his black beard!

My father and his friends enjoyed hearing these descriptions.

"What a character," my father said.

"Single-minded," added his artist friend, Mr. Samuel Morgan. "The best artists often are."

"Very much so," I added. "He usually works straight through mealtime without a break. I'd waste away if I tried that." The gentlemen nodded all around. "And after he's done for the day, he heads straight to Germania House for the evening." My father raised an eyebrow. "I followed him once or twice." I studied my shoes while they laughed at my discomfort. I'd heard what went on in a saloon.

Mr. Horace Greenly, my father's lawyer friend, cleared his throat before commenting. "Schwartz's already a frail fellow. Least we can do is make sure he eats one good meal a day."

They decided to supply a cook until Mrs. Schwarz could arrive from Germany to join her eccentric artist husband, and a handy man to do a more thorough cleaning a couple times a week.

Mrs. Mae Cooper, whose father had been a well-respected artist in the Indianapolis area, agreed to prepare food. Every day she brought lunch and dinner for Schwarz, and for me if I was there. Her daughter, Amelia, often accompanied her. I recognized Amelia from the class two years behind me. Schwarz immediately enlisted Amelia to be his young girl model in his 'Peace' display that would be on the West face of the monument. I modeled for the boy in the same grouping. A writer from the community, Suzanne Harding, modeled for the Winged Victory figure in the same display.

The handy man they hired was an elderly gentleman, Mr. Singleton, a disabled Civil War veteran, who agreed to help with the maintenance one or two evenings a week. He performed a similar function at the capitol building during the weekdays. I would often stay and help Mr. Singleton because I'm able-bodied and I enjoyed hearing the old fellow recount his war experiences.

"How'd you earn that scar?" I asked him, after only knowing him a few hours.

"Bayonet, boy. Hand to hand combat. Damn Reb had thirty pounds on me and a powerful swing. Last thing I ever saw with this eye was that blasted blade slicing down." He slashed downward with his arm, and then fingered the raised pink mark that disfigured the left side of his face.

Singleton continued to regale me with his escapades and so many point-of-death moments that I wondered how one man could have lived through that much evil without becoming permanently soured on life.

One morning, only a few weeks after I met Mr. Singleton, evil caught up with the old soldier.

I opened the workshop as usual but found a box of old metal scraps that Singleton failed to deposit on the trash pile in the alley behind the workshop. I carried the box out back and that's where I found the old man, dead, atop a pile of blood-soaked rubbish—with a mysterious symbol painted on his forehead and a slice across his throat that would never produce a scar.

The studio didn't have a phone, so I raced my bicycle through the streets of Indianapolis to our home on North Meridian Street in time to catch my father at breakfast.

"He's dead, Father. Someone killed him." I was panting and trembling and could barely get the words out.

My father rose from his chair. "Who? Schwarz?"

I shook my head. "The old man, Singleton. He's in the alley. There's blood everywhere."

He immediately phoned the police, then his physician, and

finally, his lawyer friend, Mr. Greenly. My father's influence reached marvelous lengths; I received an excused absence from school for the day, and the poor gentleman's body was photographed and removed from the site before Schwarz arrived to begin work.

Later the same morning, the police questioned me about Singleton's activities at the studio and whether he'd had any visitors. I explained what little I knew. They also questioned Schwarz, but he barely recognized the victim's name and knew none of his history. By early afternoon we'd returned to business as usual. Amelia and Miss Harding joined us after school for another modeling session. We whispered about the Singleton horror as we stood side by side in our Civil War-era costumes, speculating on whether reported animosity at the capitol building had followed Singleton and spilled over into our back alley during the night.

That evening, after Schwarz finished for the day, I swept the rooms. A folded piece of paper in the debris pile caught my eye. Thinking it might be an important receipt, I picked it up for closer scrutiny.

I stared, uncomprehending, at a sketch of a younger Mr. Singleton. The disfiguring scar through his left eye distinguished him, but he wore a Rebel uniform and brandished a whip on an emaciated Union prisoner. An arrow pointing to the prisoner was labeled 'me'. The drawing was signed George Hawking.

What type of slander was this? Who would dishonor the murdered old man in such an evil way? The same triangle symbol I saw earlier in the morning on the dead man's forehead flew at me from the lower corner of the page. It was encircled by the twisted image of a copperhead snake.

Without the powerful emotions surging through my system that had forced me to flee to my father that same morning, I had the presence of mind to study the symbol on the paper. I'd never seen anything like the triangle with the numerals three, five and seven at the internal angles and the letters KGC in the center. Whatever the secret to this code, someone had decorated Singleton's forehead with it, which made this piece of paper an important clue. I refolded it and stuffed it deep into my pocket, intending to show my father.

I finished my chores by sweeping the debris into a box and carrying it to the alley out back. I felt a chill when I recalled the gruesome sight of Mr. Singleton's body lying across this very rubbish pile. Did a man's spirit linger at the site of his death? Did the killer linger at, or return to, the site of his atrocity? I tried to shake these thoughts from my mind and hurried to throw the trash onto the mound. A movement from the back of the bin sent my heart into my throat. It was only a rat. I pretended to lunge toward it and the rodent scurried deeper into the muck.

Moments later, with my hand still shaking slightly, I locked up for the night. As I pointed my bicycle toward home, I heard the unmistakable clicking of footsteps approaching from the south. Human footsteps. As far as I knew, the murderer was still at large. Would he dare return to the scene? I hid myself and my bike in the impenetrable shadow of the thick shrubs beside the studio. As the footsteps neared, I quietly pushed deeper into the darkness. Had Singleton heard his murderer's approach? I tried not to breathe lest I meet the same fate.

When the threat eventually appeared at the door, I momentarily felt relief. It was only Mrs. Cooper. She must be coming back to pick up those dirty dishes from today's dinner. I didn't wish for her to see me cowering in the bushes, so I remained silent. But before she entered the building I heard more footsteps coming from the other direction. She heard them too and paused with her key in the lock. I could see her face from my hiding spot and she looked anxious but not afraid. Indeed, she greeted the newcomers in a manner suggesting this was not a random meeting.

"Thank you for coming," she said in a whisper. "Sam, were you followed?"

Followed? What sort of clandestine meeting was this? I could make out the silhouettes of three men but couldn't see their faces from my position.

"Greetings, Mae," the taller man said. "No one saw us."

With shock, I recognized the voice of my father's artist friend, Samuel Morgan. My curiosity kept me hidden, watchful. I stared into the darkness at the backs of the other two men. One displayed a short, round stature unmistakably that of Mr. Horace Greenly, my father's lawyer. And wherever Mr. Morgan and Mr. Greenly were, there, as expected, was my father, the third man in this strange group.

Mrs. Cooper opened the door, entered and turned on the lamp in the corner of the room. The men followed her in. The door didn't latch behind them and I crept closer to peer inside. Mrs. Cooper was leading the men to the dressing area. I took the opportunity to slip inside and hid behind the massive sculpture in the center of the studio floor.

"She admitted to bringing the drawing with her today," Mrs. Cooper said. "She must have dropped it in here when she was getting into her costume."

"Why did she even bring it?" Mr. Morgan asked, irritation evident in his voice. "You said she'd never met the Copperhead."

"She only wanted to show Schwarz her grandpa's uniform. His regiment had a unique patch. She thought it would look good on the sculpture."

"It would, too," my father said softly. "George deserves recognition in a memorial. Her heart's in the right place."

"So's yours," Mrs. Cooper said. "But you risked too much. If anyone finds Dad's drawing and puts it together…"

"I'd do it again," Morgan said. "Even if someone finds the picture, they can't tie anything to me. It'll just serve to tell the world what a traitor the old man was. Maybe we should hope it is found and makes the front page of the *Sentinel*. 'Knight of the Golden Circle in Our Midst,' or 'Beloved Artist Suffered as POW at Hands of War Criminal.' Great headlines, you must admit."

"Don't be insane, man," Mr. Greenly said. "Amelia knows you and I were at Mae's and saw the drawing. It would spell our ruin. It's enough to know the deed is done."

"Be still, you old fools, and keep looking," Mrs. Cooper said. "I don't want to regret I told you I'd found the traitor. My father loved all three of you. He won't rest any easier if you hang."

I sucked in my breath. Surely, I hadn't heard her correctly. Fear of a different sort caused a cold sweat to form on my torso.

"No one's going to hang, Mae," Morgan said. "Quit worrying. We still turn a blind eye to vigilante killings here in Indiana. I know for a fact the police will understand the clue I put on the bastard's forehead. Once they confirm it applies to this traitor, they won't look any further. Guaranteed."

"That's true, Mae," Mr. Greenly said. "After all, this monument is for remembering those who died, and we sure can't forget George. We made a vow."

They were quiet for a moment, allowing me to process their conversation. So, the KGC in the symbol meant Knights of the Golden Circle. I'd read about them in the paper. They were a much-decried cult supporting a second Civil War and the return of slavery. And I knew the expression 'Copperhead' referred to Southern sympathizers from Indiana and other Northern states. I eased the piece of paper out of my pocket and studied the face of young Mr. Singleton. I remembered his wild, unbelievable recounts of his war adventures. He'd been nice enough to me. But this concerned my own father. He and his friends couldn't be wrong about something this serious, could they? I knew who I had to protect. I slid the piece of paper with the drawing on it around to the opposite side of the statue and waited in hiding.

After a few minutes Mrs. Cooper said, "Oh, praise the Lord,

that must be it," and I heard four sets of footsteps rush to the sculpture. I heard the paper rustle as it was passed from hand to hand.

"Sleep well tonight, Mae," Mr. Greenly said after a moment. I heard some backs being slapped, the light went out, and they all left by the front door.

I sat for a while in the darkness, stunned by what I'd learned and wondered what I should do next. It didn't seem like I could do much since I'd relinquished the picture.

The next morning, I asked my father about the meaning of the symbol I'd seen on the dead man's head. He confirmed the police were looking into the KGC and Copperhead angles and it probably meant the man wasn't who he pretended to be. He studied me for a moment then said, "I wish you hadn't been the one to find the body, son."

I wholeheartedly agreed. And silently wished I hadn't been the one to find the drawing.

# # #

Five years later, Mr. Greenly waited in the back of the church to escort my lovely Amelia down the aisle at our wedding ceremony. My father and I stood side by side in the alcove by the altar and I worked up my courage to ask him about Amelia's grandfather, his old artist friend.

"Ah, George has been on my mind today. I wish he could be here." He straightened his tie and studied the top of my head.

"We were a tight circle of friends, George, Samuel, Horace and I. Enlisted together and made a pact to watch over each other's families if we didn't make it back." He let out a deep breath. "The Rebs captured George and he died in that hell hole, Andersonville, at the hands of a butcher, shortly before the war's end." My father squared his shoulders. "Our own war ended sometime later."

I remembered the drawing on the piece of paper I'd found in

the artist's studio and understood which event ended the war for my father and his veteran friends.

He smiled at me and his dark eyes met mine. "We kept our vow and watched over George's wife and little Mae. Now you're going to watch over his granddaughter, Amelia."

He pulled me into an embrace. "You don't know how happy that makes me, son."

After the ceremony, the wedding party met at Monument Circle for a photograph in front of the 'Peace' sculpture and fountain. I could see Amelia's grandfather's regiment patch on one of the returning soldiers. I could see my likeness in the boy and Amelia's in the woman. Miss Harding soared above all, miraculously without her cane, as the angelic symbol of Victory. I wasn't alone in appreciating these features and I suddenly understood that for my father, Mr. Greenly, and Mr. Moore, this monument and this wedding confirmed that justice for George Hawking and his family had been achieved: the circle was complete.

MY MEMORIES OF SUZANNE

I met Suzanne when I joined a writing group in 2004 or 2005. This amazing group met every two weeks and continues today. For years, Suzanne brought a steady stream of chapters from her first series (nine books in all) featuring an amateur sleuth/liberal arts professor. I really enjoyed this character and her world, but these stories were sadly lost upon Suzanne's death.

Suzanne carefully read each member's offering and provided a thoughtful critique. She didn't pull any punches and often provoked stimulating discussions about plot and character development. One of her signature critiques involved 'voice.' I remember she'd put her fist up by her ear and rock it back and forth, imploring us to "listen to the voice" of a particular phrase that captivated her, which meant high praise for the work under discussion.

One of her favorite authors was Sharyn McCrumb. Suzanne created an homage to this author with numerous short stories about the mysterious adventures of a small-town female sheriff in McCrumb County, Indiana. Suzanne enjoyed saying that her characters would take over the direction of the story. Well, the McCrumb County characters demanded more time and eventually evolved into novel-length romantic suspense, with four in the series published by Bella Books.

For Suzanne, good storytelling was a beautiful thing and she encouraged the short story format as a means of honing the craft. She would beam with motherly pride every time she read a particularly well-written story or one of us had a submission accepted. Her advice and critiques have been invaluable. I'm proud to have had her as a friend and colleague. She is sorely missed.

Diana Catt

FLASHES OF LIFE
DIANA CATT

Seventy-five miles following the same battered blue van with Jersey plates to the tune of the drone of big-rig tires had Kel re-thinking his fantasy. Truck driving offered monotony, not a cowboy-like adventure. At least back at the office he had a comfortable seat, coffee at the ready, and easy access to the restroom. This experiment only proved his drivers deserved a raise, not that he'd made a wrong career choice. Plus, it gave him way too much time to think about Macy. At least at the office he could find something to do the block out the painful, haunting memories.

He intended to have this truck back at his company's lot on the northwest side of Indy in two hours...or he guessed he'd just have to fire himself from driving. Ha. What a loss. Of course, the time limit was only a self-imposed deadline, he could return anytime. His mom had agreed to pick up little Alice from day care, but the boss should always strive to look good in front of his regular drivers.

The sun was setting directly over the road ahead of him. It bathed the world in a haze of orange and pink blinding light. The steady rhythm of his tires on the interstate was hypnotic. He turned the air vent to high and lit up a Winston. The smoke filled his lungs with the anticipated flavor but did nothing for the heavy sensation in his eyelids. He cranked the music up a little louder. Damn it. How do those guys do this every day? He needed another cup of coffee.

His thoughts inevitably drifted to Macy. She had meant everything to him. Not a day had passed in two and a half years that he didn't relive her death, suffer the fear she must have felt. He was obsessed with that fear. To go through that alone must have been horrible. The sourness in the pit of his stomach returned. He needed Rolaids more than coffee.

The old van in front of him veered suddenly into the passing lane to overtake a slower moving pickup. The driver didn't even bother to signal. Kel followed, pulled his semi alongside the pickup and glanced at the driver. She was wearing cut offs and a tank top. Nice.

"Must be these views that keep them awake," he thought.

She had her left foot propped up on the dash near the driver's door with her left hand tapping on her leg, keeping time to music infinitely more lively than what he was listening to.

Macy used to do that.

They made eye contact through his oversized side mirrors. He smiled and waved. She flipped him off.

Laughing, he refocused on the van ahead of him. Aw, shit. Shit, shit, shit! The van had no break lights and had slowed to make a U-turn in an emergency-vehicle-only turn around. Shit. He was going to rear end them.

He honked and stomped on the breaks. The tires squealed and jerked the cab hard to the right. Behind him, he heard the sickening sound of metal crumpling and remembered the girl in the pickup. Aw, shit. He pulled the wheel back to the left to try and stay on the road, but the trailer end started to come around.

He was in a spin on I-70, headed toward the edge of the road, and the driving course he'd taken hadn't given him the experience he needed to regain control.

The semi slid closer and closer toward the guard rail, suddenly looking too fragile to protect the steep ravine on the other side from invading traffic. In a flash, the moment he both feared and yearned for since Macy died, was upon him. He was going to die. It was clear in his mind. An accepted fact.

Instinctively, he leaned down across the seat and hung on. As the semi rolled down the ravine, he saw earth where the sky should be, felt his back and then his feet hit the roof of the cab, and then lost consciousness.

He gradually became aware of muffled voices coming from a great distance but aimed at him. He could not move; could not remember where he was. Everything was black. From his semi-conscious state, the voices triggered a memory...

# # #

I know that voice. Mom. And that one is Macy, crying. For an eight-year-old, she cries a lot. Mom is crying too. Dad is asking Macy to calm down and explain what happened. She wails about me insisting on riding Lady, my pony. That she tried to stop me.

Crazy girl. Today was perfect for riding. I mean real cowboy weather - hot and dry - just like on the cattle drives in the movies. I took a handful of corn out to where Lady grazed in the pasture. Macy stayed behind the fence issuing gloom and doom stuff about the 'mad' pony. While Lady crunched the corn, I jumped on her back. I know, I know...I should've at least put the harness on her 'cause she reached her head around and bit my leg.

Obviously, she didn't want to be ridden, so I slid off. I patted her rump and talked to her real nice even though she'd just bit me, but then she started kicking. Caught me in the stomach and doubled me over. Kicked the breath right out of me. The next kick caught the side of my face and I was lying in the dirt. Macy screamed. Mad Lady's feet continued to cut the air over my head like a wild thing.

I felt Macy grab my shirt collar and drag me out under the two-wire fence. I appreciate the kid working so hard. I'm a whole year older than her and a whole lot bigger. Had to be tough.

Just wish she'd stop crying. It's embarrassing.

# # #

The distant voices faded away. He was pulled from the depths of his memory just to the edge of reality by the wail of sirens signaling the approaching emergency vehicles. He was vaguely aware of the pain in his head before he fell back into the blackness…

# # #

"The noise hurts my head, Mom. Can they shut it off?"

"I don't think so, Kelly, but we'll be at the hospital real soon."

"Are you sure Dad's coming?"

"Absolutely. I can see him and Macy in the car behind us right now. Don't worry. He'll be there."

"Why did Macy have to come, anyway?"

"Remember? Her parents are away today and she's playing at our house? You were very lucky that young lady was there, honey. You could have been hurt much worse."

"She's not a young lady...she's just a kid."

"Um hum. Well, I'm very grateful the kid was so brave."

# # #

The siren changed pitch and pattern. The image of a fire engine floated through his mind. Other images followed. He could smell smoke, burning hair...

# # #

Dad brings the car to a screeching halt as close to Grandma's house as we can get. Fire trucks, police cars and emergency vehicles block the street. Bloated fire hoses zigzag across a yard full of people. Firefighters hustle everywhere and neighbors stand on the fringes, watching. Grandma's house looks epic. There is a gaping black hole in the roof, all the windows are broken, and flames are shooting out. Streams of water fly through the air, soaking everything.

Mom and Dad spot Grandma sitting in the back of an ambulance. She looks very old. I mean, she is old, but today she looks ancient. Her hair sticks out a funny way and she's wearing fuzzy blue house slippers.

I look around for Lucky but can't see her anywhere. Lucky is Grandma's black Labrador. I gave it to her last year for Christmas.

"Grandma! Where's Lucky? She all right?"

"Lucky?" Grandma asks, kind of in a daze or something. "Oh, Honey. I don't know. I'm sure someone found her."

Well, I didn't wait another second. I know Grandma keeps Lucky chained up out back, off the deck. She's probably hiding underneath.

"Kelly. Kel come back here," Dad yells after me. But I ignore him. I have to save Lucky.

Around the back of the house, I can see the chain. One end is attached to the railing of the deck, the other disappears underneath.

"Lucky? Here girl," I call, pulling on the chain. It burns my hands. I wrap my shirt tail around the chain and keep pulling. She must be really scared, or she'd come right out when I call.

Just then, Dad pulls me away, and into a tight hug.

"Let me go. I've got to help her," I cry into his chest, struggling against his strong arms.

"I'm so sorry, son. I'm so sorry. She can't be helped now."

It was then I notice the smells. The strong acrid smoke with definite hints of burnt hair and flesh mixed in, and I know she is gone. Poor, poor Lucky Dog.

She had to have been so scared.

# # #

The jarring sound of metal crunching pulled him back to the black unknown where strange noises, odors, and pain surrounded him. Pauses in the metallic sounds were filled with the rhythm of hands beating on glass. Through the confusion he could make out words. It sounded like "Hey! You in there! You've got to wake up..."

# # #

"Hey, Kel! Wake up!"

I open my eyes and sit up in bed. I hear someone pounding on my bedroom window. It sounds like Macy. Weird. It's midnight. What's going on?

"I know you're in there. Wake up! You've got to wake up!"

"All right, all right. I'm coming. Pipe down Macy, you'll wake up the whole damn house."

I open the window and she crawls right in! What is it with these freshmen? They think they can do anything.

"This had better be important."

Her face is puffy and tear stained. Crying again. Actually, that's not really fair to say. She hasn't done a lot of crying for a while now, I guess.

"What is it Macy?" I ask, gentler this time.

"We're moving!"

"So?"

"To Illinois."

"Oh."

"Oh? That's all you can say? This is awful. I don't know a soul in Illinois."

"But Macy…." I thought fast. "Well, gee Macy. You're a great kid. You'll make lots of friends fast. Real fast."

"Kid? Do you still think of me as a kid, Kelly Michael Haggerty? I'm only one year younger than you!"

"Well, yeah...sorry. Just habit, I guess. But really, Macy. You're one of the friendliest, best pals a guy could have. Even for a girl, I mean."

"Kelly!"

"Oh, you know what I mean."

"I don't know why I even thought you'd care." And she turns and climbs back out the window.

"Well, I don't know either!" I yell after her.

I get back in bed but can't fall back to sleep. Macy is moving! Weird. All my life she's been right next door. We live miles from any other kids and we naturally became best friends. Of course, I don't need a playmate anymore, now that it is only forty-one days until I get my driver's license. But still...weird.

And I really don't mean to hurt her feelings. Freshmen are so emotional. Hey. I'll get her a going away present! Something to remember our friendship by. I think I have some money in that metal box in the closet—the one I locked and lost the key to about three years ago. There might be enough.

I get a screwdriver and hammer and begin to beat on the metal box. The metallic echoes are sure to wake up Mom and Dad, but I have to keep after it. I have to keep beating away at that metal box, until it breaks, until I rip open the metal.

# # #

The metallic ripping noise stopped. He felt cool air bathe his body. He was so mixed up. Where was he anyway? He hurt all over now and couldn't move. He tried to open his eyes but couldn't. Did he leave the window open after Macy left? No...no, Macy wasn't here; that was a dream. He needed to pull up the covers though, he was getting cold. Why couldn't he move?

Then came a new noise. He knew this one. The steady thumping of helicopter blades, making their solitary, steady march across the sky…

# # #

So, what is this now? My twelfth air show? Dad and I've been coming together every year since I was five or so, I guess. Dad always gets these great seats. An honorary thing. Dad was a chopper pilot in the military and saved a guy's life. That same guy now runs this airport and sends Dad two front row tickets every year. But this'll be the last one for me for a while. Off to college in a week. Dad's more quiet than usual.

Here comes the helicopter brigade. This is Dad's favorite part, of course. They will land right in front of us. As they close in, the rotors whip up the air around us. Dust, air show programs, Styrofoam stuff, and heat off the engines envelop us. Like every year, Dad puts his arm around my shoulders.

# # #

The arm around him wasn't his father...and the pain from the touch shocked him back to the present.

"He's alive! Get that stretcher down here," a voice called.

Still trapped in darkness and confusion, his pain erupted to a new level of intensity.

"Take him up," the voice yelled.

He moved upward, and twirled around and around...

# # #

"What?" I ask, as the hand from behind twirls me around. The room is crowded. It's my fraternity's first big party of the school year, and as always, it's a blast.

I stare at the beautiful woman who is holding my shoulder and fall under the spell of that smile I remember so well.

"So, Kelly Michael Haggerty, aren't you going to say hello?"

"Macy? My God! What are you doing at Purdue?"

"I'm still only a year younger than you, Kel. Don't act so surprised. I hoped I'd run into you tonight."

"Why didn't you call me or something? How'd you know I'd be here anyway?"

"Mom. You know, she got it from your mom. Told me. Here I am."

I grab her and hug her tight. "It's so good to see you again!" And it is. I suddenly realize how much I miss her, having her to talk to, to be my friend.

She hugs me back. We move to the dance floor and stay in each other's arms, talking, laughing, twirling…twirling.

# # #

The twirling stopped. The stillness was filled with pain. Slowly, the sounds of nearby traffic filtered into his consciousness. He tried to focus on the other sounds as well. There were voices. He could distinguish the words.

"Who's going by Lifeline?"

"The girl from the pickup, for sure. Don't know about this guy yet. We'll have his vitals by the time you get the girl on board."

"Right."

Pain, in his arm. Voices again.

"Shit. His pulse is dropping fast…"

# # #

"Her pulse is dropping fast."

"What? What's happening, Doc?"

"Get him out of here. Now! Prep her for surgery."

"Wait, let go of me! I've got to help her! I have to be with her."

"Come on, Mr. Haggerty. You'll only be in the doctor's way. You can't be of any help in here."

The nurse pushes me out through the automatic double-wide doors of the delivery room. Something is wrong. Gut wrenching, panicky wrong. I struggle with her but there is no choice. I can't stay. The last thing I see in Macy's eyes is fear. She doesn't want to be alone. Doesn't want to have our baby alone.

"I love you, Macy," I yell, praying she can hear me. "I'll be right here!"

The doors woosh shut behind me.

# # #

He opened his eyes and saw an unfamiliar woman staring at him. He looked beyond her to the ceiling and scanned the brightly lit room. Obviously, a hospital room, but why?

"Well, well," the woman said. Her name tag read Suzanne H. "Glad you could finally join us, Mr. Haggerty."

He struggled with the first words. "Where am I?"

"You're at Methodist Hospital. Been here for two weeks."

"What?"

"Can you remember anything?" the nurse asked.

He closed his eyes and thought. Yes. He remembered a lot. A lot about Macy. Eventually fragmented memories of the wreck entered his mind.

"The girl in the pickup. What happened to her?" he asked softly.

"Released two days ago, I believe."

"Good."

He was quiet for a long time. The nurse was heading out the door when he finally spoke again.

"I wasn't afraid," he said.

"What?" the nurse asked, returning to his side.

"I knew. I mean I knew for sure that I was going to die, and I wasn't afraid."

"Well, you're going to pull through now."

"I always thought she must have been so afraid. That if I'd only been with her it would have been easier somehow. But we die alone, don't we?"

"Don't worry about dying, Mr. Haggerty. The doctor says you'll be fine."

"Yes," he smiled. "I'll be fine. It's good to be alive again."

DEAD IN THE WATER
JANET WILLIAMS

Getting the old guy drunk was the easy part. Maneuvering his 280-pound frame down his driveway and plopping him into the passenger seat of his oversized SUV took all the strength we could muster.

"Tell me again, Kate, why we don't just shoot this S-O-B?" Ainsley gasped as we wobbled to the car with the barely-conscious Andrew McMillen lurching back and forth between us. S-O-B was the closest thing to a swear word I ever heard Ainsley utter.

"Because we ain't gonna kill him. Just make his life a little miserable." That low, raspy voice was Max, who stood by McMillen's vehicle.

"A bullet to the head would be easier," Ainsley said, breathless and wheezing as together we staggered across McMillen's driveway with our victim weaving between us.

Easier on paper, like we do in the stories we write. But not in real life.

McMillen was barely conscious, and we struggled to get him to the car door before he slipped into the black sleep of Vodka tonics and Ambien Ainsley had fed him after she got him home from the bar where she picked him up.

"Let me help," Max said as he hobbled across the remaining few feet of pavement and reached for the arm Ainsley held, but I waved him off.

"Max, get your bony ass back here. You'll give yourself a heart attack," Eva said from the driver's side of the SUV.

"Oh for Chrissake, you didn't worry about my heart last night."

"Max! Just get back here," she hissed before lowering her voice and adding, "or there won't be any tonight."

Ainsley and I smiled at each other. Max and Eva's fling at Second Chances Village was the worst kept secret. Chastened, Max returned to his station at the car door. Eva was right. Max, though recovered from the heart attack he had last year, was a shell of his ex-Marine self and wouldn't have been much help.

"We need your help getting him into the car," I said as we neared the passenger door.

McMillen let out a loud belch as he slouched toward me, giving me a whiff of whiskey and garlic.

"Next time maybe skip the Italian dinner," I said, stifling a gag.

"We goin' for a ride baby?" McMillen slurred.

"Yeah, baby," she replied as she smacked his cheek.

He groaned and a smile crossed his lips as he threw his head back, almost knocking us off balance.

"Hey, baby, just one more," he slurred, pressing his lips together as he leaned toward Ainsley and attempted to plant one on her. He missed and got a mouth full of her blond hair as it flowed in the breeze.

"E-e-e-w-w-w." Ainsley pushed his face away and his head lobbed toward me.

"I told you to tie your hair back," I said.

"Sorry, but no man was ever seduced by a ponytail."

Eva pulled off the knit cap she wore and handed it to Ainsley. "Here, shove your hair up under this. Less chance of leaving evidence."

As Ainsley tucked her hair into the cap, Eva plucked a blond strand from McMillen's coat.

"How 'bout you, sweetie?" McMillen leaned forward to Eva and tried to pucker up, but his mouth went slack. Probably the pills Ainsley put in his last drink. I feared that in another minute, he would be out.

"Just how many of those pills did you give him?"

"Two. Maybe three. I dunno, he's a big guy," Ainsley said, stumbling in her spike heels.

"Geez, Ainsley, we don't want him to O-D. Just dope him up a little," I said.

"Well, you weren't there and he was getting grabby." She shivered.

I should have stopped us. I wish I'd stopped us. We were acting like characters in a bad Elmore Leonard knock off—Ainsley, demure teacher by day, blond seductress by night; Max, the ex-Marine, Vietnam vet and obligatory muscle; Eva, the grandmotherly widow with a little of Bonnie Parker in her soul; and me, Kate, the accountant and brains of this gang of misfits.

It was colder than any of us expected that late November night. The wind whipping through the trees blew away the last remnant of autumn's leaves as dark, billowy clouds blotted out the moon and stars. The air smelled damp and musty and I thought I heard a distant rumble, heightening my sense of urgency and dread. I'm a numbers person and usually cautious so I should have taken the weather and our struggles to march our victim to his car as signs that we should call the whole thing off.

But I didn't. Instead, I double-clicked McMillen's key fob to unlock his SUV, a mammoth black behemoth, and Max opened the passenger door.

"C'mon, Andy, we're going for a nice little ride," I hissed as he placed one foot into the car and flopped onto the seat, sprawling over the console and halfway onto the driver's side.

"We're going bye-byes?" He slurred his words.

"Not yet, old man, not yet," I said, dragging his body back to the passenger side as Ainsley pushed from the driver's seat. Max lifted his other leg and shoved it into the vehicle.

"Smaller guy next time," Ainsley said as she slumped in the driver's seat and I handed over the car keys. She adjusted her cap as she checked herself in the rearview mirror. "All right, how do I start this thing?"

"You slide that black key fob into that slot right there in the dashboard," Max said, indicating the spot. Ainsley slid it into place and the SUV purred to life as she pressed the starter button. That's what you get with a big-ass luxury SUV—not a growl but a purr.

"OK, I think I got this," she said, reaching under the front seat to move it forward.

"No, no, no," Max and I said almost in unison.

"You can't change the seat. Any fool cop could figure out that a guy as big as McMillen wasn't behind the wheel," Max said.

"Then how am I supposed to reach the pedals?"

"Edge of the seat," Max said. "You're tall enough to reach then."

She rolled her eyes, scooted forward and shifted the vehicle into gear.

"Wait a minute," I said. "Seatbelts."

"Seatbelts? We're framing a guy for drunk driving and you're worried about seatbelts?" Ainsley rolled her eyes but still grabbed hers and locked it into place. I took the belt on the passenger side and reached across McMillen's bulging belly and a chest so flabby he could have worn my grandmother's bra. I struggled for a moment to find the other end and then click, the seatbelt was secured.

"A lot of women pay big money to get boobs that size," I muttered, as I backed out of the vehicle.

McMillen snorted, grabbed my arm before I was completely out and slobbered, "Yeah baby, let's do it."

"You ain't doin' nothing." I pulled my arm from his thick fingers. It dropped like a slab of meat and his head slumped to his chest. Finally, he was out.

"Is he dead yet?" Eva called from across the driveway.

"No! He's not dead yet. We aren't killing him, remember?" Ainsley said.

Max took Eva by the hand and led her to my car, the vehicle the three of us had arrived in after Ainsley had maneuvered McMillen into driving her to his place from the restaurant. She had signaled that the drugs and booze were working from inside the house by flicking the front porch light. Now, she had one final task.

"Don't forget. You're stopping on that hill by the big oak where the road makes a sharp left turn," I said before closing the passenger door.

Ainsley nodded, but I could see she was gripping the steering wheel so tightly her knuckles bulged through her leather gloves.

As I walked toward my car, Ainsley called out, "Kate, I…" I turned and Ainsley shook her head. "Nothing. See you there." Her voice quivered. She looked scared and small behind the wheel of the massive vehicle.

Another sign. It's easy to say now that I should never have let her do the driving or that this was another point where I should have called the whole thing off. But I didn't.

# # #

Was it four months ago? Five? Suzanne, the leader of our erstwhile band of writers, hobbled into our meeting in the coffee shop of our neighborhood bookstore, pounded her cane on the floor and launched right into a rant.

"Can you believe it? Probation? He just got three years

probation! He stole millions, the swindling son of a bitch! He cheated dozens of people and… probation?"

Suzanne slammed her notebook onto the table and yanked out a chair, dropping her body into the seat. She was oblivious to the people at tables surrounding us who had gone silent. One teenage boy a couple of tables over even cast a sideways glance at this slight hurricane of a woman.

"Slow down, woman," Max told her. "What the hell are you talking about?"

Max had missed our last couple of meetings—his heart. He never heard Suzanne raging about the developer who took the deposits of hundreds of families to build homes on farmland about fifteen miles southeast of Indianapolis. Geyser Estates. That was the name of the project of affordable homes on thirty acres on a branch of the White River. But it was more than that. These weren't mere houses. These were dreams. Dreams of people who would be owning their first homes, dreams of people wanting their own piece of paradise on a river in the country.

That developer, Andrew J. McMillen, dug a few foundations on the land and even started building one or two houses, but never made any real progress. After a couple of months, he started dodging his customers, who bombarded him with calls demanding to know when their homes would be ready to move in. And they almost always used the word home because that was what McMillen sold them—the dream of owning their own home.

After months of blowing off the men and women who entrusted their life savings to him, McMillen declared bankruptcy. The feds began investigating him on all kinds of fraud allegations and eventually, after more than two years of limbo, McMillen was charged with fraud and embezzlement. It would be another year and a half before he went to trial and as a result, several families went bankrupt and at least one family ended up temporarily homeless.

Suzanne would have been angry on general principle that after a trial and a guilty verdict, McMillen was sentenced to probation by the 60-something judge. A judge, who by the way, once belonged to the same country club as the crooked developer. But her fury was amplified—that doesn't even begin to do her rage justice—because a dear friend had lost her life savings investing in Geyser Estates. Every last penny that would have bought her and her disabled son a home of their own gone while McMillen got to keep his estate, that luxury SUV and all of the trappings of a life built on the life savings of hundreds of working-class families.

I'm not quite sure how we went from her fury, which we all shared, to a plan. I think Eva might have been the one to say something about us being good at plotting murder on the written page so maybe we ought to try it in real life.

"Good one, Eva," I said as we all laughed.

"Just think about it a minute. How many murders have we plotted?" she asked.

"Let's see, maybe a couple dozen," Ainsley said.

"A lot of people would love to kill that crook, but it's easier on paper than in real life," Suzanne said.

"But we can fantasize," Max said.

Yes, we could fantasize and get our revenge in our imaginations and in our stories.

"Isn't he always at that steak place downtown? We could poison his cocktail sauce. That stuff is so potent he'd never notice," Eva said, flashing a wicked smile.

"Yeah, remember that poison lady from last year's Magna cum Murder conference? Didn't she talk about arsenic and cyanide?" I asked.

"Killing without blood, guts or gore," Ainsley said.

"Something slow and painful. Give him a taste of the pain he put his victims through," I said.

We pondered the possibilities for a silent moment.

"Naw, wouldn't work," Suzanne said.

"Why not?" Eva asked.

"We'd never be able to get close enough to poison his food. Besides, too many ways to get caught," Suzanne said. "It's not like you can waltz into your neighborhood drug store and buy any of those drugs. No, no. Just too complicated."

We sat silently for a few more minutes as we pondered the many ways we all had committed murder—on the written page.

"Then why not just plug him? A couple shots in the heart and he's kaput," Eva said, pointing her finger like a pistol at Max. "Bang, bang."

"Too cliché," Suzanne told her. "Every two-bit crook uses a gun. Besides, they're noisy, they make a bloody mess, bullets can be traced. We can be more creative."

"There are guns that can't be traced," Ainsley said slyly, opened her handbag to reveal a small silver snub-nose revolver. A Saturday-night special.

A gun? Ainsley, the demure teacher, actually had a gun?

"What the hell you going to do with that?" Suzanne whispered as she leaned closer to Ainsley so nobody at the surrounding tables could hear.

"Oh, nothing. I don't even have bullets. But after our gun class last year I decided to see how easy it would be to buy one off the street. You know, research for one of my stories. And it was pretty easy. Just told the dad of one of my first graders that I needed a gun and he hooked me up with a guy in Haughville. A hundred and fifty bucks and it was mine."

"Let me see," Eva said, reaching across the table for the weapon before Ainsley closed the purse.

"What the hell were you thinking?" I asked.

"She's always telling me that I need more authenticity in my writing." Ainsley nodded in Suzanne's direction, then told her directly, "You're always telling me my writing sounds like a school girl's idea of a murder."

Suzanne let out a deep sigh. "Well, get rid of it before you get into trouble." And when she saw Ainsley slump into her chair, she added, "You could have gotten yourself hurt or killed."

Ainsley opened her mouth to speak but stopped. She knew this wasn't an argument she could win.

"I've got one," Max said, breaking our uncomfortable silence. "We could lure him to one of those half-built houses and knock him off there. Then set it on fire."

There was a certain poetic justice to the idea, but fire? When no one responded Max made a jabbing motion with an imaginary knife and said, "We get him quick. Make it look like a robbery."

Suzanne shook her head. "Where? How? Haven't you learned anything from TV cop shows?"

Reality check. "Security cameras," I said.

"We could make it look like suicide," Ainsley said. "Maybe make it look like one of those autoerotic asphyxiation things."

"Auto what?" Eva looked confused.

"Autoerotic asphyxiation," Ainsley replied. "It's when you…"

"No, no, no." Max covered his ears as he cut her off.

"Look at this like you're writing a short story. Keep it simple," Suzanne said after a moment. "What if you just wanted to make your villain suffer a little? Not kill him, just humiliate him."

And so, we began.

Suzanne was off on her book tour, but the rest of us met every other week and worked out the details of our plot. Ainsley, Eva and Max researched McMillen's life and habits, putting details to the broad outline of his life that we heard about from television news. I dug through court records where we got more details about how he used the down payments from would-be homeowners not for construction supplies but to finance his life of luxury, including frequent dinners at a local Italian restaurant where he'd wine and dine his female companions.

We had good stuff but didn't have a real plan until Ainsley suggested that she pick up McMillen at that bar. From there it was nothing to go from plotting what could have been a pretty good story to planning a crime.

I kept track of the planning in a small notebook: Ainsley picks him up and then lures back to his own place; Max, Eva and I follow from a safe distance; Ainsley drugs him with some Ambien she got from Eva; we get him to his car so we can stage a drunk driving accident. A semi-conscious McMillen would be found drunk and incoherent in his own wrecked vehicle after we called the police. Our hope was that his probation would be revoked and he'd wind up in prison where he belonged.

Maybe if Suzanne had been there that final evening we wouldn't have taken the next step—turning revenge fantasy fiction into a real life story, a story that didn't turn out as planned.

# # #

Ainsley let the car drift slowly down McMillen's driveway and it wasn't until she hit the isolated two-lane road a quarter mile from the house that I heard her give the engine a little gas.

Max, Eva and I followed in my gray sedan, a car like thousands of others. Eva had climbed into the front seat, insisting that Max sit in the back because she said she didn't want to miss a thing.

We stayed far enough back that the rear lights were a blur in the distance. I hadn't quite realized how foggy it had become that evening until after a few minutes Ainsley and her companion faded out of view.

"You better step on it," Max said as he leaned over my shoulder. "They're getting too far ahead."

"Sh-h-h. Let her drive," Eva snapped. "You're always telling people how to drive."

"That's because you…" Max started to say when I interrupted and told them both to shut up. I might have used profanity because Eva gasped and Max sat back with neither saying another word. For the next ten minutes we crept along the winding road in thickening fog until we came to a rise in the hill and the dim red taillights came into view. A gray cloudy mist swirled in the headlights.

I pulled to the side of the road a good twenty feet behind McMillen's vehicle and told Max and Eva to stay in the car while I helped Ainsley, who was standing beside the open passenger door. Our passenger was still out cold, slumped sideways over the console.

"Andy, hey Andy," I said, reaching across and slapping his cheek. I was hoping to wake him up enough to walk him around to the driver's side but all he did was release a loud snort.

"We'll have to drag him across. You pull and I'll push," I told Ainsley.

"Yeah, that'll work," she replied, trudging to the other side.

If I thought our staggered march to the vehicle was difficult, it was nothing compared to trying to drag McMillen's hefty mound of flesh across the console. I struggled to lift his legs and swung them around so I could push them and the rest of the body into the driver's seat. Ainsley grabbed his arm and tried to reach around to his other armpit to get a little more leverage.

"Ick," she said, pulling her hand away. "It's all wet and it smells."

"Just pull!"

Ainsley reached under his arm again and as she tugged at the body, I held both legs and pushed. He edged over the console, the belt on the back of his pants catching on the plastic rim of a cup holder.

"Can't we just leave him here?" She was breathing hard.

"Not if we want to be sure he gets busted and gets his ass thrown into prison," I grunted, still pushing.

"Let me help," a voice behind said, startling me and causing me to drop the legs. It was Max. I hadn't even heard him get out of the car.

"Max, your heart, we got this," I said.

"That's what I tried to tell him." Eva was right behind him. "I can do this." She tried to push past Max and grab one of the legs, but Max swatted her back.

"I got this!" I never heard Max quite so angry. "Besides, these girls aren't doing so well on their own."

Max looked shrunken in his hunting jacket and I wasn't sure how much help he could be but I sighed and said, "All right. Max, you take one leg and I'll take the other. Eva, see if Ainsley needs any help."

"It can't hurt," Ainsley said.

Eva trotted around to the driver's side, reached around Ainsley and grabbed the hair on the top of McMillen's head. She shrieked as the brownish-gray mass came off in her hand. Fake, high-quality fake, but fake nonetheless, like everything else about this guy.

"He's bald as Max's bottom," Eva said, examining the clump that resembled a bird's nest in her hand and then tossing the toupee onto his face.

Max grunted and pushed harder. Eva and Ainsley grabbed McMillen's jacket to pull and we did make some progress until his bulging belly got stuck at the gearshift. As Ainsley reached across to grab his belt, she leaned onto the gearshift. It was only when the SUV began drifting forward that we realized in bumping the gearshift, Ainsley knocked the vehicle out of park.

"It's moving," Ainsley shrieked as she and Eva fell back from the SUV, sliding into the muddy slope. I felt Max drop McMillen's leg as he backed away from the vehicle, which was beginning to move a little faster. The force of the SUV moving forward made me lose my balance and as I tried to grab onto the door, it swung back and hit me on my forehead, sending me flopping backwards into the mud.

"Help me! I think I broke a hip," Eva called out.

I saw Ainsley struggle to her feet, the mud making it hard for her to get traction in her heels, and attempt to stumble after

McMillen. The driver's side door clipped the tree and banged shut as the vehicle continued to roll down the slope to the river below. I managed to stand up and watch the SUV lumber down the hill, tumbling back and forth as it rolled over tree roots, small gullies and rocks. I started after it, slipping and sliding as I struggled to run through the mud. I kept thinking maybe, just maybe if I moved fast enough, I could stop it. But the SUV kept rolling and rolling and rolling until it reached a cliff about five feet above the water. I could have sworn it slowed or might even have stopped as it moved to the edge and I thought for a second that I might be able to catch it. But just as I got near the vehicle, it tumbled forward into the water below. I slid onto my knees as I got to the edge in time to see the rear bumper disappear below the water.

By then, Ainsley had caught up with me and we both stepped over the edge and slithered on our backsides to the water's edge. Neither of us could see the SUV because the night was as black as the water and the fog was denser closer to the river.

"He'll drown!" Ainsley cried.

Tell me something I don't know, I thought as I tossed my jacket onto the bank and stepped off the edge of the bank into the water, immediately sinking to my chin. My legs cramped in the icy water and I figured I had just a couple of minutes to try and pull McMillen from the wreckage. So I took a deep breath and went below the surface, but between the particles of dirt that stung my eyes and the inky water I couldn't see a thing. The SUV seemed to have vanished. I popped my head above the water and took a big gulp of air.

"Oh, God, I thought you drowned, too!" Ainsley sounded frantic.

"I-I can't find him. I can't find him!" I think I was crying, but I'm not sure.

"Let's get out of here," she said, stretching out her hand to help me out of the water.

We scrambled up the hill to find Eva and Max still sprawled on the ground, neither of them able to get up. Together, Ainsley and I pulled Max to his feet and we went to see about Eva, who was still moaning about her hip.

"You really think you broke it?" Max asked softly. She moved her legs and shook her head no as he added, "Come on, take my arm and we'll help you up."

With Max holding her hands, Ainsley and I got behind Eva and gently pushed her to her feet. She groaned a couple of times but as she stood, she said she was shaken but not seriously hurt.

"I-I think I can walk OK," Eva said as Max helped her limp to the car.

"Let's get the hell out of here," I said to Ainsley as I wrapped my jacket tighter. I was still dripping wet and my jacket did little to keep me warm. My sneakers squished in the mud as I walked.

It was then that Ainsley discovered she was missing one of her shoes, yellow with a spike heel, that had disappeared into the muck. She turned to go back after it, but the fog had thickened as it began to rain, at first a drizzle and then a little harder.

"Shit! We'll never find it in this mess," I said, taking her by the arm to stop her from plunging down the embankment again.

"But my shoe," she said. "It could be evidence!"

Yes, she was right. Evidence. My stomach did a couple of flips as the rain streamed down my face and into my eyes, almost blinding me. Black streaks of mascara ran down Ainsley's cheeks.

"Oh, God, what else will they find down there?" I sounded panic-stricken as I looked to the dark, murky water below.

"I don't know. Maybe fingerprints? Hair?" Ainsley was sobbing

"Did you kiss him and maybe leave a trace of lipstick?"

"E-e-e-w-w, no."

"Quick! Get up here!" It was Max behind the wheel of my car, barely visible behind the dashboard. When we didn't move fast enough he yelled in a harsh whisper, "Just get your asses in here."

We stumbled through the leaves, twigs and mud as the rain turned into a downpour. When we reached the car we fell into the back seat. We had barely closed the door when Eva yelled at Max to pull out, but I grabbed his arm to stop him from shifting.

"Wait a second," I said, pulling my phone from my purse and punching in numbers—nine...one...But before I could hit the last digit Ainsley grabbed the phone from me.

"Are you crazy? We just killed a man!"

"Yeah, yeah, but we should get the police or someone out here," I said, reaching for my phone.

"Oh honey, ain't no way he survived in that muck," Eva said.

"Okay, then what? Just go on like nothing happened?" I didn't expect an answer.

"So, we call the police and tell them what? How do we explain this mess? Or the fact that it doesn't even look like McMillen was behind the wheel?"

"And he's full of those drugs you gave him," Max said.

"And how will I explain my missing shoe? Or even being in this get up?" Ainsley asked, referring to the slinky white dress with gold sequins, now clinging even more tightly to her body and spattered with mud.

"Let's just get out of here!" Max said, jamming the car into gear and hitting the gas. For a brief, panicky moment the front wheels spun in the mud before it jerked forward and onto the road.

I grabbed my phone back from Ainsley and said, "Suzanne. We'll call Suzanne. She'll know what to do."

An hour later we were at Suzanne's place, a two-acre ranch-style home about ten miles from McMillen's failed development. She bought it after her series became a bestseller.

"You did what?" I will never forget her tone, somewhere between anger and bewilderment when we finished telling her what happened.

We were gathered around her fireplace, the burning logs warming and drying us while a bottle of Jack Daniels she had won at a writing conference steadied our nerves.

"So you," she said to Ainsley who was now wrapped in a frayed plaid blanket, "you were supposed to seduce him?"

"And drug him," she said in a voice so low I could barely hear her.

"And the plan was to go barefoot?"

"I, I lost a shoe in the mud." She pulled her bare feet under the chair and turned to face the fire so she wouldn't have to look Suzanne in the eye.

Suzanne sighed, the disapproving kind of sigh that spoke volumes about how much we disappointed her. I felt like I had let down my favorite teacher. I suppose I had. I could guess what she was thinking—what fools we were to leave so much evidence behind. But she didn't say that. She didn't need to.

"Where's the mate?" Suzanne asked.

"In her car," Ainsley replied, nodding in my direction.

"And Max, you were supposed to be the getaway driver?"

Max shrugged and I signaled with a limp wave of my hand that getaway driver was supposed to be me.

"Eva, what about you? You just go along for the ride?"

"I was the lookout," she said indignantly as she perched on the edge of her seat.

"The lookout," Suzanne said as she turned to me. "And you? You the mastermind of this fiasco?"

I shook my head then said, "It was kind of a group effort. I just kept track of the details." I pulled my notebook from my bag and Suzanne grabbed it, flipping through the pages.

"So you're telling me it's a conspiracy?"

"Not exactly. More like a team-building project," I replied, realizing as soon as I spoke how ridiculous that sounded.

"You should have known better." She looked straight at me. "Stopped this gang that couldn't shoot straight from getting in over their heads."

"This was your idea," Max told her and when she turned toward him he quickly diverted his eyes.

"As a writing exercise! I never told you to go out and kill the guy." She tossed the notebook into the fire and we all watched as the pages curled and burned.

That wasn't exactly our plan, I wanted to tell her, but instead I asked her if she had any suggestions for what we should do now. She didn't answer right away and instead stood up with the help of her cane and walked to the window where she pulled back the curtain to watch rain pelt the window.

"You've got one thing working for you," Suzanne said with a sigh. "You don't have to worry about tire tracks with all this rain."

That made me feel a little bit better until she said, "Besides the shoe, what else did you leave behind? Fingerprints? Hair samples?"

"I cleaned up before we left his house," Ainsley said.

"What about his car?"

"I don't think we left anything," Ainsley said.

"What do you mean you don't think you left anything? That's the kind of stuff that can get you caught," Suzanne said. "We can only hope the muddy water and rain washed all the evidence away."

"We wore gloves," I said while Ainsley reached for her purse to show Suzanne the leather gloves she wore. But when she opened the bag she let out a gasp that chilled all of us.

"What? What?" I asked as all attention turned to her.

"My gun! It's gone!"

"Your gun? You took a gun with you tonight?" I might have been yelling I was so shocked.

"I thought I told you to get rid of that thing," Suzanne said, pounding her cane on the floor.

"I-I, didn't know where to dump it."

"So you decided to take it with you?"

Ainsley nodded.

"We'll all go to jail now," Max said. "My golden years, in the slammer."

"I can't go to jail. I just can't. They'd take away my teaching license." Ainsley burst into tears.

"Getting kicked out of the teaching profession is the least of your worries," Suzanne said as Ainsley's crying softened into a whimper.

That felt like a gut punch. Max grabbed Eva's hand and held on tightly while Ainsley dropped her purse to the floor. I swallowed hard as I struggled to keep from getting sick on the spot. As we sat silently considering our limited options, the sound of thunder crashing and rain pounding the side of the house shook us. When the lights flickered and went out for a few seconds, Max muttered, "Divine punishment."

"Punishment, hell. This storm is a big fat gift," Suzanne said.

A gift?

After a moment she started barking orders like a drill sergeant: "You, Ainsley, get rid of the mate to the shoe you lost. Kate, there's a pay phone at that little market not too far from the accident. Use an old rag or something and call 9-1-1 and tell them you saw a car driving crazy heading up that road. And then all of you go home, get cleaned up and never breathe a word of what happened tonight to anyone."

That's just what we did.

# # #

Weeks passed as each of us settled into the rhythm of our lives. We resumed our critique sessions, sticking to the pieces each of us submitted for review and avoiding any discussion of what we termed our "misadventure." Suzanne had missed the next several meetings because she was traveling to promote her latest novel, but the rest of us never spoke of the incident. Too scared.

Meanwhile, I anxiously checked internet news sites for information about the accident and the fate of Andrew McMillen.

There was nothing. No reports of an accident and nothing about McMillen at all.

Until nearly two months later.

It was late January and I was doing what had become a perfunctory scan of local internet news sites when a headline caught my attention: "Police seek developer who cheated hundreds of their life savings." I clicked on the story and sure enough it was about McMillen and how friends, family and former business associates hadn't seen or heard from him since around Thanksgiving. Now his probation officer and police were looking for him. The article, noting that more than $50 million in assets had never been accounted for, implied that McMillen skipped town with his bounty.

"That scumbag," was my first thought before I remembered that I was partly responsible for his disappearance. But why no mention of the SUV and what happened to his body? I couldn't afford to be too curious so I kept my thoughts to myself.

After that a few small articles popped up on various internet news sites speculating about what happened to the developer who bilked so many people. Then, in early March, a local television station did one of their crime beat stories and announced a $10,000 reward had been posted for McMillen, now assumed by everyone to be a fugitive. I wasn't sure if I should be relieved or more nervous because I figured it was only a matter of time until his car and body surfaced.

I only had to wait a week. The top story on every local news station was about how police had caught Andrew McMillen at a regional Indianapolis airport as he attempted to board a private jet that would take him out of the country. A dispatcher recognized him from the crime beat alert and turned him in for the reward.

He was alive? When? How? And what would he tell police about us?

Then, a couple of days later, the SUV literally surfaced more than 20 miles from the spot where it had plunged into the water. A rainy fall had given way to a dry spring and a birdwatcher spotted the vehicle where it washed up near shore. A bald eagle had perched on the roof.

Meanwhile, as we nervously waited for the police to come knocking on our doors, we kept meeting because Suzanne insisted we maintain our regular schedules. But there were no police and little word of McMillen in the news.

Until late May, six months after our mishap, when we were gathered for another critique session. Thankfully the coffee shop section of the bookstore was deserted except for Max, Eva and me when Ainsley raced in and slapped the daily newspaper on the table.

"Did you see this?" she asked breathlessly, brushing her hair, now auburn, away from her face.

"Yeah, what about it," Max said as we read the headline at the top of the page, which was something about a legislator taking kickbacks from a gambling lobbyist.

"No, not this," she said, pointing to an article at the bottom of the page. "This!"

"Developer violates probation, sent to prison," Ainsley read aloud the headline, over a photo of a ragged and bearded Andrew McMillen in handcuffs.

"What the hell," I muttered as we gathered to read the story.

A Marion Superior Court judge ordered developer Andrew McMillen to prison where he will serve the full three years of his sentence for theft and fraud after violating terms of his probation.

Chief Deputy Prosecutor Angela Bascomb told Judge Evan Bonaroti Tuesday that McMillen was caught trying to flee the country with a forged passport and a suitcase filled with more than $1 million in cash.

"Mr. McMillen attempted to stage his own death by driving his SUV into the White River before disappearing last Thanksgiving," Bascomb said. "We believe he intended to fake his own death and start over in Uruguay."

McMillen, 57, was convicted in October of swindling dozens of families who had bought houses in his development on the city's far eastside. Most of the money that was supposed to be used to construct the homes in his Geyser Estates plan went to funding his opulent lifestyle, which included works of art, collector's cars and expensive jewelry.

"Your honor, we believe that Mr. McMillen was with a woman when his Lexus SUV went into the water," the prosecutor said. "Investigators found a single spike-heeled shoe in the wrecked vehicle. What's more, they discovered a handgun in the front seat, a gun that was used in a liquor store holdup in downtown Indianapolis two years ago. We're investigating his connection to that crime as well."

"Lies, all lies!" McMillen yelled as he was dragged from the courtroom in handcuffs to begin his life behind bars. "They were trying to kill me!"

"Says here McMillen's lawyer claimed his client was in hiding because he was convinced hired killers were after him," Eva said, grinning. "Imagine, thinking we were hired killers."

"Maybe if he hadn't tried to flee with the suitcase full of cash," I said and I let out a long sigh of relief.

"Well, damn, we did it. We got that cheating son of a bitch right where he belongs," Max said, as he rose and headed for the coffee counter. "This calls for a celebration! Chocolate chip cookies for all."

Yes, we did it, I thought as I stared at McMillen's photo and wondered how he managed to escape a watery death or how the current carried that behemoth of an SUV twenty miles downstream. We'll probably never know and I was okay with that.

As we munched our cookies, Suzanne stormed into the bookstore and banged her cane against the table as she dropped into the chair next to Ainsley.

"Book tour end early?" I asked.

She didn't answer but went straight into a rage: "You remember that executive at the Pearl Foundation who assaulted his assistant?" We nodded. "Well, can you believe it! He got a suspended sentence for indecent exposure and get this, he gets to keep his job!"

"That scumbag," I said.

"Ain't no justice in the world," Max growled.

"Somebody needs to shoot the son of a bitch," Eva said before turning to Ainsley. "Too bad you still don't have that gun."

"Yeah, too bad," Ainsley replied before she got a twinkle in her eye and a wicked grin spread across her face. "But who needs a gun when you have Ambien."

START IN THE MIDDLE – MY MEMORY OF SUZANNE

I was proud of the first piece I wrote for the class I took with Suzanne Harding at the Indiana Writers Center in 2015. I really nailed the assignment, showing character through action, creating a sense of place in my short piece of fiction, the first I'd written in a decade or more.

I was newly retired and signed up for her classes at the Writers Center because I always planned to write fiction, but work had kept me busy, or so I told myself. It was now or never.

Suzanne returned the assignment to me with a line drawn through what I thought was a brilliant opening with a scribbled note, "Your story starts here."

But what about that wonderful opening?

"Start in the middle," Suzanne told me.

Sigh. I had to set aside my own ego, not an easy thing. But I was in her class to learn how to write fiction and so, after thinking about her suggestion, I returned to the story and rewrote it, starting off with the passage she suggested. And yes, the story was better.

That is how Suzanne taught her classes. She got straight to the point and didn't mince words when she knew what wasn't working in a student's story. And her message about starting in the middle resonates with me to this day.

From that class she invited me to be part of *In Mysterious Company* and I am grateful. I have become part of a wonderful writing group that still bears the imprint of its founder, Suzanne.

I followed her advice for the story I wrote for *Circle City Crime.* I started in the middle. I hope I took her lessons to heart and more than anything, I wish she were here to read it.

Janet Williams

EXIGENT CIRCUMSTANCES
MICHAEL ELDRIDGE

Hangover? There had to be a better way to describe how David felt. Head filled with flaming death maggots. Rancid brain farts exploding from nose. Walking dead with no hope of actually being dead.

How long had it been? Five, no, six years sober? All of it wiped away in one long blurry night of, what? He had no idea. He only knew that he felt hungover.

David swung his legs over the edge of the bed and tried to sit up. He fell face-first on the floor into something wet and smelly. Vomit. The odor hit his senses like a sledgehammer. His stomach spasmed, heaving up more of the already substantial volume of puke on the rug next to his bed.

Barely conscious, he lay marinating in his sour body fluids for minutes before gaining the strength and presence of mind to roll onto his back. His effort was rewarded by several solid objects that threatened to poke holes in his body. The pain stimulated action. He sat up, drew his legs to his chest, wrapped his arms tightly around them, and pressed his face against his knees. He managed to avoid falling back to the floor.

After a few minutes of deep breathing, he felt stable enough to attempt moving. Standing was out of the question. He crawled to the bathroom. Grabbing the edge of the tub, he pulled his body up and over the side and tumbled in. He landed with his head near the drain, his legs dangling over the opposite end.

The effort caused the room to make a couple of revolutions around his body. He closed his eyes and concentrated on breathing. Slowly the room stopped spinning. Another deep breath and he reached up with both hands and opened the faucets.

"Jesus Christ."

The words exploded from his mouth as he desperately tried to get from beneath the torrent of icy water threatening to drown him. More by reflex than design he pulled his legs into the tub and sat up. The room spun and he felt sure he was about to be sick once again. He squeezed his legs to his chest and closed his eyes.

"Come on man, breathe. In through your nose and out through your mouth. Again."

When the spinning stopped, he gently opened his eyes and released his legs. Then ever so slowly he turned until he could reach the knob that controlled the shower. The spray from the shower rained down on his head, shoulders, and back. Gradually he pushed his feet along the bottom of the tub until he was sitting with his legs fully extended.

Avoiding any sudden moves, he began to unbutton his shirt. Then he carefully pulled his arms from the sleeves. He pushed, rather than threw, the wet vomit-soaked shirt to the bathroom floor.

The water was becoming uncomfortably hot. He slowly turned his body until his feet were at the drain. He adjusted the faucets until the water was warm and then leaned forward to allow the water to flow over his head and back.

The threat of the room spinning out of control seemed to have passed. He winced as he ran his hands through his hair and over his face. His face was sore and sported several cuts that bled as he touched them.

"What the fuck?"

As he looked at his bloody hands, he realized his knuckles were also cut and swollen. Closer examination revealed a large purple blotch spreading across the left side of his ribs. The area was tender. It hurt when he breathed.

Clinging to the side of the tub for support, he carefully raised himself to his knees. The room tilted but did not spin. After a few beats, he unbuttoned and unzipped his pants. He slid his pants and briefs down to his knees and gently sat back on his bare ass. He removed his pants, underwear, and socks, leaving them where they fell.

He surveyed the damage. His knees were skinned and there were cuts and bruises on both legs. The big toe of his right foot was swollen, purple, and bent toward the left.

As the fog lifted from his mind, pain slithered in. The water from the shower was running pink with blood and he was again feeling nauseous.

"Well, Davey, my brother, seems like you really got yourself in the middle of it this time."

Slowly, slowly he stood up and stepped out of the tub. He grabbed a towel and tried to dry his head. He seemed to be bleeding more and the room took another circuit. One deep breath and he headed for the hall.

"I should call 911," was his last thought before he collapsed.

# # #

Jim Tetum looked around the newsroom. "Has anyone heard from Cox this morning?"

"No? Jill, what about you? Any idea where our wayward reporter is this morning? I'll tell you where he's supposed to be. He's supposed to be here groveling and apologizing for missing his deadline on the congressional bribery piece."

"Sorry J.T. Haven't seen him for a couple days," Jill said.

"Unless you're putting the finishing touches on a Pulitzer-worthy story, go find him," Jim said. "You vouched for him. I'm holding you responsible."

"Ok, I'll give him a call."

"Great idea, why didn't I think of it? Wait. I did. His phone's going to voice mail. It has been since 6:00 a.m. You want to be an investigative reporter? Then investigate. Move your butt from your desk to your car and go find him. Unless he's dead or on life support, drag his sorry ass in here. Now." Jim stomped back to his office.

# # #

Jill climbed the three steps to David's door.

"You better not be sleeping off a bender," she said as she knocked. She waited a moment then knocked harder.

"Damn it. Wake up," she said as she hammered and then kicked his door.

"Glad I didn't give the key back after you moved in." Jill unlocked and opened the door. "Ready or not here I come. Hope you're alone and decent."

She stepped inside, looking around the living room. "David? Where are you? J.T. is on the warpath. If he doesn't get your scalp, he'll take mine."

The draperies were closed, casting the room in half light. She flipped on the ceiling light.

"God, you're still such an incredible slob. This place should be condemned. What is that smell?"

She headed for the bedroom. What she saw stopped her in her tracks.

"God, David. What in the world happened to you?"

As she knelt next to his naked body, she grabbed the towel lying next to him and wiped blood from his face. When he didn't respond, she grabbed his shoulder and shook him.

"David, wake up. Please wake up."

She tried and failed to find a pulse.

"You son-of-a-bitch. You better not be dead. Damn it all, wake up."

She reached for her cell phone, but it wasn't in her jeans' pocket.

"Damn. It's in my car. Let's see if you still leave your phone on the coffee table," she said, heading to the living room.

It was on the coffee table. "I hope you haven't changed your password."

She unlocked the phone and dialed 911. After the call, she automatically slipped David's phone into her jeans' pocket.

# # #

The apartment seemed to shrink as more and more people—police, fire department, and ambulance crew—crowded in to treat and investigate. When they arrived, Jill was struggling to catch her breath. She tried to leave, but a large policeman told her to sit on the couch and stay there until he had time to take her statement.

Finally, the medics wheeled David out to the waiting ambulance. Jill stood and started to follow them, but the cop blocked her path.

"Are you a family member?"

Jill struggled to maintain her emotions.

"Ah…no. I'm…I don't know what I am," she said through the tears that were now streaming down her face.

The policeman picked up a box of tissues from the coffee table and handed it to her.

"Sit down. Take a deep breath. Tell me what happened here," he said as he guided her back to the couch.

"I need to go with him."

"First, you need to tell me what you know about this situation." He took a notebook from his pocket.

"What's your name?"

"Jill. Jill Baker."

"Ms. Baker, may I see your identification?"

Jill took her license from the little cardholder she carried in her pocket. She handed it to him, and he made notes.

"What's the victim's name?"

"Victim? His name is David. David Cox."

"Is this his apartment? Do you live here?"

"Yes. No. Yes, it's his apartment. No, I don't live here."

"But you have a key?"

"Yes, I have a key." Jill took another tissue and blew her nose.

The policeman waited until she recovered her composure.

"What's the nature of your relationship?"

"We're friends. We work together. We used to date." She took a deep breath. "I've known him for years. He recently moved to Indianapolis. I helped him find an apartment and move in. That's how…why I have a key."

"Can you tell me what happened here?"

"I have no idea. David didn't show for work this morning. He wasn't answering his phone. Our editor sent me to check on him."

The policeman made some notes, then focused on her eyes as though he was reading her thoughts.

"When you arrived, was the door standing open or was it unlocked?"

"It was locked. I knocked. I banged on the door and shouted. When he didn't answer, I unlocked the door and found him there in the hall…naked and bleeding." Jill grabbed another tissue.

"And, then?"

"And then…and then I called 911. I thought he was dead."

"Do you know of anyone who would want to harm him? Did he have enemies or issues at work?

"No. I don't know of anyone who would do this, and no, he wasn't having problems at work.

"As far as you know," he said. "Where do you work?"

"We're both reporters for the *Indianapolis Telegraph*."

Jill stood. "Is there anything else you need?" she asked as she stepped toward the door. "I'm going to the hospital now."

The cop raised his hand signaling her to stop. Then he reviewed his notes and told her she was free to leave.

"If we start a criminal investigation you'll likely hear from a detective," he said, stepping aside to let her pass.

"What do you mean if you start an investigation? He certainly didn't assault himself. Clearly there's been a crime and it needs to be investigated." She pushed past the officer.

Once outside, Jill checked her pocket for her car keys and phone. One of the EMTs said they were taking David to Methodist Hospital. She started her car and headed downtown. At the first stoplight she took her phone from her pocket. She was surprised to find it was David's. Her phone was lying in the passenger seat. She picked hers up and called her office.

"J.T. This is Jill. I found David."

"Good. Now drag his lazy ass in here."

"Can't do that, Chief."

"Why the hell not? Is he passed out drunk?"

Tears welled in her eyes. "No. He's in the hospital."

"What the…what happened?

"I don't know. When I got to his place, I found him on the floor. He was unconscious. It looked as though someone tried to beat him to death."

"Jesus. Did you call the cops?"

"No. I thought I'd leave him there and see what happened. Of course, I called the cops."

"Okay, okay. Sorry. Where are you now?"

"I'm on my way to Methodist. Should be there in about fifteen minutes. I'll call you when I have details."

As she drove, she realized there might be something useful on David's phone. She pulled into a drugstore parking lot, picked up David's phone, and unlocked it.

"It's a good thing you're too lazy to change your code regularly," Jill said, checking David's recent calls. David was working a story about a corrupt politician from Florida. He'd made a lot of calls to Florida and Washington D.C. Next, she looked at his email. He had half-a-dozen unopened messages, all advertisements. One more possibility, texts. Finally, success.

A text from a Nathan Frost sent yesterday at 9:13 p.m. said: "We need to talk." David's response: "I don't think we have anything to talk about." That was it.

Frost. That name sounded familiar, but Jill couldn't place it.

"I'll check you out later, Mr. Frost," Jill said as she drove from the parking lot and headed for the hospital.

# # #

Jill had worked the crime beat so she knew her way around the hospital. She also knew that she'd have to lie about her relationship with David to get any information on his condition, let alone be allowed to see him.

Jill went directly to the Hospital Administrator's office. At the reception desk, she gave her name and asked to see Susan Good.

After a brief phone conversation, the receptionist indicated a row of chairs, "Ms. Good will see you in a moment," he said.

Before she could sit down, Susan entered the room, arms spread wide.

"Jill. It's wonderful to see you." She gave Jill a warm hug.

"It's good to see you, too. I hope I haven't come at an inconvenient time?"

"Your timing is perfect. I don't have anything on my calendar for another hour. Frank, please hold my calls," Susan said as she ushered Jill into her office.

Before Susan could offer her a seat, Jill blurted, "I need information on a patient."

Susan frowned as she motioned Jill toward a chair. "What's this about?"

Jill took a deep breath and tried to hide her worry behind a timid smile. "I'm sorry. I found a friend beaten unconscious in his apartment. I'm afraid the police will write it off to a misadventure,

'Known alcoholic falls off the wagon, gets into a bar fight, staggers home, and collapses.'"

"Could that be what happened?"

"No. I've known David for ten years. He had problems back in D.C. about six years ago that nearly ruined him. He was a first-class investigative journalist. Everyone thought he was in line for a Pulitzer. Then he was accused of fabricating a story about a prominent congressman."

"Couldn't he prove he didn't do that?" Susan asked.

Jill struggled to hold her emotions in check.

"He could have, except a fire at his apartment destroyed all his work. Then the Twitter-verse exploded with accusations that he'd been embellishing stories for years. Some suggested he was guilty of flagrant plagiarism. There was even one thread that accused him of setting the fire to cover his many sins."

"What did he do?"

"There wasn't anything he could do. D.C. is a tough town. He lost his job and was threatened with legal action. After he was fired, he spiraled into depression and started drinking. Drinking heavily. I'm ashamed to admit I lost confidence in him. I left him when he needed me most." Her voice broke and tears flooded down her cheeks.

Susan rushed to her side. "It'll be okay. Look at me. We'll figure this out. Tell me what you need."

Jill wiped her tears with the back of her hand. "I need to know exactly what the doctors found. I need to know how much alcohol was in his blood and if there were drugs present. I need details of his injuries. I need everything they tell the police but won't tell me."

"Do you suspect it has anything to do with what happened in D.C.?" Susan asked as she sat in the chair next to Jill.

"I do. There are rumors that the politician David investigated is considering a run for the White House."

"That's a long time to hold a grudge."

"Not for this man. Over the years he's ruined at least a dozen people who opposed him. Three committed suicide and two more simply disappeared without a trace."

"I understand you're concerned, but I don't know how much I can get for you. I'm pretty limited by HIPAA regulations."

"Please. Just get what you can. I'll take anything you can find out. I'm afraid whoever did this will try again."

"I'll do what I can, but I think you should take your suspicions to the police," Susan said as she stood and walked to her desk. "I'll call you with what I find out. Wait a second. There's a writer whose been interviewing the hospital staff for a book she's writing on racial inequality and hospital access. She's well-connected and seems to have an in with nearly every department. Her name is Suzanne Harding. Here's one of her business cards."

# # #

Jill went to the emergency room and learned David had been moved to the ICU. At the ICU she ran into hospital bureaucracy. The duty nurse grudgingly admitted David was there and that he was in critical condition. No. She couldn't see him. No. She couldn't talk to his doctor unless she was his spouse or close family member.

Her phone rang. The nurse at the desk pointed to a sign on the wall that read 'No Cell Phone Calls in This Area.'

Jill glared at the nurse as she answered the call.

"Hello, this is Detective Bruce Osgood with the IMPD. Is this Jill Baker?"

"Yes." She headed toward the elevators at the end of the hall.

"I need to speak to you about the statement you gave to my officer this morning at the apartment of Mr. David Cox."

"Okay. What do you want to know?"

"I need to speak with you in person. Would it be convenient for you to meet me at my office?"

"I guess. I'm just leaving the hospital."

"In that case, could you meet me in the hospital cafeteria? I'm having a late lunch. We can talk here if you can spare the time."

The detective's tone made it clear refusing wasn't an option.

"I'm just about to get on the elevator. I can be in the cafeteria in about five minutes. How will I know you?"

"I'll watch for the woman with the worried face who's looking for a cop she doesn't want to talk to," said Osgood as he broke the connection.

"Wise ass," Jill said as she punched the first floor button.

# # #

Jill entered the cafeteria, eyes forward at a steady walk. She hoped the cop wouldn't spot her. "It'll serve you right if you don't know I'm the woman you're expecting," she said under her breath.

No such luck. A tall man in a rumpled navy suit rose and waved her over. Then he picked up the trash from his lunch and dropped it in a nearby receptacle. They both reached the table at the same time.

He extended his hand.

"Ms. Baker? I'm Detective Osgood. Please have a seat," he said, gesturing to the chair opposite.

Osgood referred to an iPad laying on the table.

"According to the officer who took your statement, you and Mr. Cox are friends and you both work at the *Indianapolis Telegraph.*"

Jill sat down. "That's correct."

"I understand that when Mr. Cox failed to report for work you went to check on him. Is that correct?"

"Yes," Jill said, suddenly determined not to cooperate.

"What else can you tell me?"

"Nothing beyond what I told the officer." Jill stared intently into the cop's eyes.

"How about more details on how you know Mr. Cox?"

"I've known David for a long time. We used to work together at the *Washington Post*."

"I see. Were you close?"

Jill set her jaw and amped up intensity. "Yes. At one time we were very close."

"And now? Now you're just friends who happen to work at the same newspaper?"

"That's correct."

He referred once more to his iPad. "And you just happen to have a key to his apartment?"

Jill didn't respond.

"Is that true?"

"Yes, it's true, and no, we aren't friends with benefits."

Jill tried unsuccessfully to read his iPad screen.

Osgood took a deep breath and released it in a long sigh.

"Ms. Baker we have a very ambitious administrative assistant assigned to the robbery homicide division. She's especially talented at researching individuals on the internet as well as other official databases." Osgood turned the iPad so Jill could see.

"As you can see, Mr. Cox has a long and checkered past with the police and other institutions."

Jill studied the screen. Someone had pulled together an in-depth profile of David's past, and presented it in a neat outline format. It was all there—the scandal, the accusations of fabricating stories, plagiarism, and the apartment fire.

There was also a record of several arrests for drunk and disorderly and driving while under the influence. Near the end, there was an arrest for assault on a Mr. Nathan Frost for which David was not prosecuted. The charge was withdrawn.

Frost. I knew I remembered that name. He was the fixer for Congressman Tripper.

"Well," Osgood said. "Do you have anything to add?"

"Like what?"

"Do you think this is the latest misadventure in Mr. Cox's life?

Or, do you believe this is a crime associated with his past?" Osgood reclaimed his iPad.

"You should take a hard look at ex-congressman Jake Tripper and his man Nathan Frost. You'll find them both in that bio you have on that iPad."

"That's ancient history. Have you anything recent?"

"If you're asking me if I believe that after six years of being clean and sober, David suddenly fell off the wagon and went looking for a fight, the answer is no. Absolutely not."

"Do you have an alternative explanation?" Osgood asked, mirroring her unblinking stare.

"I suspect someone, maybe someone from David's past, got into his apartment and attacked him. I think they wanted to kill him."

"I'll remind you that the door was locked. There was no sign of forced entry and there were no obvious signs of a struggle," Osgood said as he crossed his arms.

"What about Frost?"

"What about him? The assault charge was dropped when Frost disappeared. No victim, no case." Osgood made a what-do-you-expect shrug.

"So, what are you going to do?"

"Until Mr. Cox wakes up, there isn't much we can do. There're no witnesses to a crime and there's no reason to believe Mr. Cox wasn't the cause of his own troubles."

"And, if he doesn't wake up?" Jill asked.

"That won't improve the situation. I suspect we'll end up with an unsolved suspicious death." Osgood put the iPad into his briefcase. "If there are any developments we'll be in touch."

"What if David were a white man? Would that put his attack in a different light?" Jill asked, not bothering to hide her outrage.

"I'm going to pretend you didn't just accuse me of bigotry."

"What if I told you Nathan Frost tried to arrange a meeting

with David last night? Would you pretend that's not a significant piece of information?"

"How would you know that?"

"From David's phone. I used it to call 911 and stuck it in my pocket."

"That phone could be evidence. I'll need you to turn it over to me, now."

"I don't have it with me. Even if I did, how can you call it evidence when you don't believe a crime has been committed?" Jill asked.

Osgood stepped close to her, close enough that she could feel his body heat.

"There was a text from Frost. It came in at 9:13 p.m.," Jill added.

Osgood's voice turned from disappointment to condescension.

"Very well, Ms. Baker. What was the text?"

"'We need to talk.' To which David replied, 'I don't think we have anything to talk about.'"

"That must sound incriminating to a reporter hungry for a front-page story. To me, it just sounds like background noise. Not very interesting. However, I want you to surrender that phone," Osgood said, extending his hand as though he expected her to hand it over right then and there.

"I told you, I don't have it with me."

"In that case, I'll give you until tomorrow morning to produce it. If you don't, I'll send someone to remind you of the seriousness of withholding evidence."

Osgood turned and headed for the exit.

"Remember. Phone. Tomorrow. No excuse."

Jill retrieved the business card Susan had given her. She pulled out her phone and punched in the number.

# # #

Jill sat at a table in the 86th Street Barnes & Noble. She was lost in thought staring at the uneaten oatmeal-raisin cookie as though the pastry held the answer to all her worries. Suddenly someone pushed the chair opposite out from the table with the tip of a well-used cane.

Jill followed the cane from tip to handle and found herself staring at an elfin woman with close-cropped gray hair and a piercing stare.

"Jill? I'm Suzanne Harding." The woman extended her hand in greeting. When Jill stood to take it, she was surprised at how strong Suzanne's grip was. Suzanne released Jill's hand and turned toward the Starbucks counter.

"I'll get something to drink and then we can talk," she said as she made slow progress across the floor.

Minutes later, Suzanne settled carefully into the chair opposite Jill. "Now, tell me your story."

Jill recounted all that had happened.

When she finished, Suzanne asked, "What do you want me to do?"

"I need to get the inside story on my friend's condition—what the hospital told the police about it. Was he drunk or had he been drugged? Did it appear he was in a fight, or the victim of an attack?"

Suzanne nodded.

"First, you need to give Osgood the phone. He's no Dick Tracy but he can be mean when his precious authority is challenged," Suzanne said, pulling a notepad and phone from her shoulder bag.

"I understand, but he's an asshole who couldn't care less about yet another attack on a black man," Jill said.

"I agree he's a long way from being colorblind when handling cases. Plus, he's a few months from retirement so he's not about to change now."

"I'll give him the phone, but then what?

"We'll go around him. You eat that cookie while I go make

some calls."

When she returned, Suzanne referred to the notes she'd made.

"Here's the scoop. David's still in ICU. He's been placed in a medically induced coma to allow his brain time to heal. Beyond that, he has three broken ribs, a busted nose, and several fractured bones in his hands. And, he has a broken bone in the big toe of his right foot."

"So, he was in a fight," Jill said, the disappointment clear in her voice.

"Not so fast. First there was only an insignificant amount of alcohol in his blood and a very significant level of drugs. It's unlikely he could have stood on his own, let alone fight."

"So, he was attacked. But where? There were no signs of forced entry and it didn't appear there had been a struggle."

"Best guess, it was in his apartment. There was no fight. Just an old-fashioned beatdown. He wasn't supposed to live," Suzanne said as she returned the notepad to her bag and stood to leave.

"That's it? What should I do?"

"Not much you can do. I've raised a flag with someone higher up in the police department food chain and she's agreed to put an officer on David's hospital room. That should protect him. As for you, I suggest you step back. If this Frost character is the perp, he might come looking for you. Keep your phone handy and call 911 at the first sign of trouble."

###

Jill sank into her living room couch. The events of the day still echoed in her brain, when there was a loud knock on her door.

"If that's you, Osgood, I'm filing a harassment complaint," Jill yelled as she jerked the door open.

The was a man standing in the hall outside her door. "Who are you? Do you work for Osgood?"

The man took a step forward, planting his foot just over the threshold, effectively preventing her from slamming the door in his face.

"My name is Nathan Frost. May I come in?" he asked, stepping inside her apartment and pulling the door closed behind him.

That's the problem with third-floor apartments. No back door. Jill backed away.

"What do you want?"

"I'm an acquaintance of David's. I want to reconnect with him, but I understand he's in hospital. Tell me how's he doing?" Nathan walked over to her couch and sat down.

"Not well."

"Do you have any idea what happened to him?"

Nathan's voice sent a chill up Jill's spine. Her nervous reaction was embarrassing. Suddenly, more than anything else, she needed to pee.

Jill took a tentative step toward the bathroom door. "Please, excuse me, but I need to use the bathroom."

"By all means. Take your time. I'll still be here when you return."

Jill hurried to the bathroom, barely avoiding wetting her pants.

"Now what do I do?" she asked herself. "I can't stay in here all night, there's not even a lock on the door."

Before she could make a decision, Nathan opened the door and stepped into the small room, placing himself directly in front of her. Jill had never felt so vulnerable in her life.

"I'll bet you're wondering if I was the one who tried to kill David," he said as he allowed his gaze to wander over her partially exposed body.

Jill's mouth was so dry she couldn't manage to make a sound. The best she could do was shake her head slightly from side to side.

A cruel smile spread across Nathan's thin lips.

Jill stiffened, but resisted the urge to cover herself or to scream.

"You're not very smart, are you? You're in kind of a compromising situation. Let's be honest. Right now, I own you."

He looked hungrily at her bare thighs and legs.

Jill looked directly into his eyes.

"What do you want?"

"It doesn't matter what I want. You will do it. You will do it and beg for more," he said as he leaned ever so slightly forward. "Get on with your business so we can go somewhere more comfortable."

Jill summoned her last bit of courage and quietly reached for toilet paper. She made no attempt to cover up as she cleaned herself. Then she reached down and slowly pulled up her panties and slacks and fastened her belt.

"That was a good preview," Nathan leered.

She raised her finger in a wait-a-moment gesture and turned her back on him as she flushed the toilet. Then she casually slipped her hand into the upturned opening of a large conk shell resting on the toilet tank.

"Quit stalling," Nathan ordered.

"Okay," Jill spun around and delivered a right cross to the side of Nathan's head that would have made her self-defense instructor beam with pride.

Nathan gasped and started to reach a hand to his injured face. He never made contact. He collapsed to the floor, his sightless eyes staring at Jill's feet.

"That's for David," Jill said as she stepped over his lifeless body.

MY SUZANNE HARDING TRIBUTE

During the relatively short time I knew Suzanne, she left an indelible mark on my approach to writing. She stressed that while writing is a solitary pursuit, every writer needs to be a member of a writing community. In my case, she insisted that my strength was as a storyteller. "Tell the story and then fill in the niceties of grammar, voice, and style," is the advice she gave to me.

In each of the stories in this anthology Suzanne makes a cameo appearance. As you meet the many faces of the fictionalized Suzanne, you'll be left with a vision for the actual Suzanne as seen through the eyes of the people who remember her with love and affection. Enjoy.

Michael Eldridge

DEAD GUY ON DECK
D. B. REDDICK

I knew it was going to be a bad day when I turned onto East Vermont Street and spotted a half dozen cop cars with their red and blue lights flashing brightly. I quickly brought my '94 Cadillac Deville to a complete stop, rolled down my window and asked the young cop directing traffic what was going on.

"There's been an incident up ahead," he replied. "Please move along, sir."

As I put my car back in gear and carefully steered around the cop cars, I glanced in my rearview mirror to see what had happened, but the sun wasn't up yet. I knew one thing though. This kind of thing typically doesn't happen in my 19th century Lockerbie Square neighborhood.

Three blocks away, I found a parking spot on North College Avenue and trudged back to my house on East Vermont. That's when I noticed several people milling about on the front yard of the two-story Italianate home owned by my next-door neighbors, Daniel Washington and Matthew Malone. Maybe something happened during their annual all-night Halloween bash.

"Thank heavens, you're here," Matthew shouted when he

spotted me. He then carefully strutted across his lawn in a full-length red-sequined gown, stilettos and a dark brown wig that had slipped slightly down his forehead. "You'll never guess what's happened."

"Your guests didn't like your Celine Dion outfit."

"No, there's a dead guy on our deck."

"A what?"

"A dead guy. Nobody paid any attention to him until the party began breaking up an hour ago," Matthew said, grabbing my arm and steering me towards his fenced-in backyard. "Nobody remembers talking to him. He was an obvious party crasher."

Once in the backyard, I noticed a middle-aged guy dressed in a dark blue windbreaker with the words "medical examiner" scrolled across the back of his jacket. He was leaning over a guy sitting upright in a lawn chair. The guy was dressed in a dark grey suit and he was wearing a Richard Nixon mask.

"Oh, goody," Matthew said, clapping his hands gleefully. "We haven't missed it."

"Missed what?"

"The big reveal. The medical examiner looks ready to remove the dead guy's mask. We'll finally find out who he is. I'm dying to know who dresses up like Richard Nixon for Halloween. It's so seventies."

A second later, the medical examiner carefully removed the mask, and Matthew screeched in my ear. "Oh, my God, it's Michael Pearson."

# # #

It took another hour before Matthew calmed down and I learned that Michael Pearson was a local real estate developer. Matthew wanted us to drive by Pearson's office to see if anybody there knew where their boss had been last night.

"It's not even seven o'clock yet," I snapped, glancing at my watch. "His office won't be open. Besides, I have a splitting headache from listening to all the folks who called into my radio show overnight. I'm going to bed."

"But Charley, we need to find out who did this. If word gets out, the city may deny us future party permits. And, a story in the *Indianapolis Star* could ruin Daniel's chances of becoming a partner at his law firm. They're deciding on his promotion next week. You want us to continue having parties and to see Daniel become a partner, don't you?"

"Of course, but I really can't help you or Daniel without some sleep first."

"Okay, I'll give you until noon."

# # #

Matthew is a man of his word. The clock radio on my nightstand read 12:16 when I heard him unlock the front door to my Queen Anne house. I inherited it a year ago from my uncle, William O'Brien. As a close friend and neighbor, Matthew has a key.

"Are you up?" Matthew shouted before entering my bedroom. He was holding Bruce, the Maine Coon cat who came along with the house. It was a package deal.

"I am now," I said, tossing off my covers.

"Good. I'm raring to go," Matthew said. "We've got to find out who killed Pearson. After you went home to bed, I called everyone at the party to see if anyone remembered Pearson. My friend Roger thought he showed up with two guys dressed in matching black suits, sunglasses and earpieces. The Secret Service look-alikes were holding up Pearson by his arms before they dropped him in the lawn chair."

"Who knew your party was a convenient place to dump a dead body? Did your friend say anything else?"

"No, but before the medical examiner carted Pearson away, I noticed some reddish smudge marks on the knees of his expensive Armani suit and Gucci loafers."

"What does that prove?"

"Maybe Pearson spent some time last night at his new condo project on North Senate Avenue. It's behind schedule. He was always complaining about it when I worked as a temp in his office a few months ago."

"Won't it look suspicious if we suddenly show up there?"

"Don't worry, Charley, I have a plan."

# # #

Thirty minutes later, Matthew and I pulled up in front of Pearson's three-story, red-brick condo development on North Senate Avenue. From the outside, I could see how Pearson might have ended up with dirt on his suit and loafers. The front yard was a sea of mud. The only way into the unfinished building was a foot-and-a-half wide wooden plank that rested precariously on top of the mud pile.

"So, what's your plan," I asked Matthew again.

"Hold on, you'll see."

A moment later, an attractive brunette in her mid-thirties stepped out of a blue minivan that she parked in front of my car.

"You must be Matthew Malone," she smiled and extended her hand. "I'm Trish Stephens, the building's realtor."

"Yes, I know," he replied, "and this is my life partner, Charley O'Brien."

Wait a minute. Life partner?

"You're both going to love living here," Trish gushed, as she turned and carefully walked across the wooden plank in her four-inch stilettos.

Matthew and I followed behind her. I thought about pushing him in the mud for his life-partner remark, but I didn't. Once across the plank, Trish unlocked the building's front door. It opened into a tiny lobby. We then walked down a brightly lit hallway to a beautifully furnished two-bedroom model unit in the rear of the complex.

As Trish dazzled me with superlatives about the granite

kitchen countertop and the fixtures, Matthew slipped away to look for any clues into Pearson's death.

When Trish finally finished delivering her spiel twenty minutes later, she whirled around from the stain-less steel kitchen range, smiled and asked, "Can you see yourself and Matthew fixing romantic candlelight dinners here, Charley?"

"I'm not sure," Matthew said as he wandered into the kitchen from one of the bedrooms. "The kitchen's very lovely, but I'm afraid the master suite isn't."

"Whatever do you mean?" asked Trish, a quizzical look on her face.

"Once we fit our king-sized bed in there, we won't have any extra space for that mirrored sitting table my cousin, Suzanne Harding, recently gave us. And, Charley, you know how much you love moisturizing in front of that mirror after your evening shower. No, this isn't going to work. I'm sorry, but we're leaving."

Matthew grabbed my arm as we quickly left the condo, leaving Trish behind in the kitchen with her mouth wide open.

"What was that all about?" I asked Matthew after we made it across the wooden plank to my car.

"Sorry, Charley, but I needed an excuse to get us out of there. I didn't find any clues into Pearson's death. Suzanne's makeup table was the first thing that popped into my head."

"And that moisturizing bit…?"

"Sorry, again," Matthew said, letting go of my bare arm. "But you really should think about using some lotion. Your skin feels like sandpaper."

# # #

We had only driven a few blocks when Matthew pulled his cell phone out of his pants pocket.

"Who are you calling?" I asked.

"Roger, the guy who spotted Pearson with the fake Secret Service agents. Maybe he's remembered something else."

While Matthew chatted away, I steered my car through the

drive-thru window at White Castle on South Street and ordered six cheeseburger sliders. I was famished.

"Why do you persist in eating that stuff?" Matthew asked as he put away his phone. "They'll clog your arteries."

"I'm hungry," I said, trying to swallow my fourth cheeseburger. "Did your friend have any new information?"

"He said the agents looked so much alike that he couldn't tell them apart."

"Hmmm… maybe they were twins," I said, biting into another cheeseburger.

"That's it, Charley. You're brilliant. They must have been twins."

"Come to think of it, I remember some middle-aged twins knocking on my door last month," I said. "They were trying to get me to sign a petition."

"Yeah, it was the Wilson twins," Matthew said. "Wayne and Wade. They knocked on our door, too. They were carrying a petition to stop an apartment complex from being built across the street from their Italianate house. Throw away those cheeseburgers, and let's check out that place."

I ignored Matthew's advice and quickly devoured the last slider on our drive to North College Avenue. I stopped my car in front of a rundown, two-story Victorian home in the middle of a huge empty lot. The house appeared ready for demolition to make way for the apartment building.

"What should we do now?" I said, letting out a tiny belch.

"Let's check the front door and see if a building permit is attached. That will tell us who owns this property."

Matthew and I carefully walked up the broken brick sidewalk that led to an equally dilapidated wooden front porch.

"This place looks like it could fall down on its own," I observed.

"It belongs to Michael Pearson," Matthew said as he turned

away from the front door. "The name on the permit is Pearson Property Developers."

"Think he was here last night instead of at his condo development?" I asked.

"Let's find out. The front door is unlocked."

Matthew and I stepped inside. The front hallway was covered in a thick coating of reddish looking dust.

"Looks like nobody's lived here for some time," I said.

"Kind of spooky, isn't it?" Matthew replied. "This would have been a great place to hold our Halloween bash. Let's check out the living room."

We walked into a large room to the right of the front hallway. Some sunlight was seeping through the dirty picture window, but it was hardly enough for us to make our way around the room without bumping into the antique furniture.

"This is where it must have happened," Matthew said, pointing to a spot in the corner of the room.

"What?"

"Where Pearson was killed. The dust has been disturbed. I also see tiny specks of blood. And, I bet the fireplace poker lying over there was the weapon used to kill Pearson."

"How clever of you, Mr. Malone."

Matthew and I whirled around to see a tall, skinny guy dressed in khaki pants and a red flannel shirt standing before us. He had a pistol in his hand.

"It's Wayne Wilson," Matthew said, turning and muttering his name in my ear.

"No, I'm actually Wade Wilson. My eyebrows are thicker than my brother's. But I just texted him. He's on his way. In the meantime, what are you and pudgy doing here?"

Pudgy? Those sliders weren't that fattening.

"This is my neighbor, Charley O'Brien," Matthew said, quickly coming to my defense. "He's a local celebrity. Charley hosts an all-night radio talk show on WZMN-AM. You've probably heard of him."

"Can't say I have," Wade replied. "I don't stay up late, but you didn't answer my question. What are you doing here?"

"Trying to figure out how Michael Pearson was murdered. And, something tells me that you know what happened to him."

"What's all the commotion?"

Wayne Wilson had stepped into the living room. "What are they doing here?" he asked, giving Matthew and me the once over with his dark eyes.

"They're nosing around, trying to figure out what happened to that bastard, Michael Pearson," Wade said.

"Well, we can fix that," Wayne said. "Give me a minute to think of something."

I didn't like the sound of that. Normally, I enjoy taking a nap on Saturday afternoons to catch up on the sleep I lose during the week from working all night. Something told me that wasn't going to happen today.

"Let's take them to the basement," Wade finally said, waving his pistol at us. "We'll take care of them there."

The basement was twice as dusty as the upstairs living room. I gagged at the sight of the mold creeping up the basement walls. Hundreds of cobwebs also hung from the floor joists as we carefully made our way down the creaky wooden basement steps.

"Tie up the gay guy with that rope lying in the corner," Wayne instructed his brother.

"Excuse me, Mr. Wilson, but I don't think that's a good idea," I said, staring directly at Wayne Wilson. "If you're not intending to shoot us, and I thank you for that, then you'll need a better cover story if the cops eventually find our bodies."

"What do you have in mind?" Wayne replied, looking at me suspiciously.

"Tie me up instead of Matthew. That way, it will look like his partner, Daniel Washington, discovered us down here. He became angry. Tied me up, hit Matthew over the head with one of the boards lying over there, and then set the house on fire."

"Say, that's not a bad plan, mister."

"I thought you'd like it. You guys can then make an anonymous call to the cops and tell them to contact a realtor named Trish Stephens. She'll tell the cops that she showed Matthew and me a new condo earlier today, and how we were planning to move in together."

"But aren't the cops still going to investigate Pearson's murder?"

"Yeah, but you can lie to them. Tell them you spotted Matthew and Pearson flirting at the Halloween party, and Matthew's partner killed Pearson in a fit of rage."

"That sounds really good, Wayne," Wade said. "It lets us off the hook for Pearson's murder, gets rid of these two guys, and we'll become heroes for stopping the apartment building from being built and destroying the homey character of our neighborhood."

"Tie up the fat guy, and keep an eye on the other one," Wayne said. "I'll run across the street and grab that gallon of gasoline in our garage. I'll be right back."

Once Wayne left, I suggested that Wade tie me up in the corner of the basement. That would give Matthew a chance to text Daniel without Wade noticing what he was doing.

Five minutes later, Wayne returned with a red plastic container full of gasoline. He began splashing the contents around the basement. Once he finished, Wayne made sure I was securely fastened before he began arguing with Wade over who'd whack Matthew over the head with a board. That's when I interrupted them.

"Guys, do the only fair thing, and let Matthew flip a coin," I said. "He carries a lucky silver dollar in his pocket."

"Who wants to call it?" Matthew asked, pulling out his silver dollar.

"Heads," Wayne spoke first.

"You always call heads," Wade said. "I want heads."

"Make it four out of seven flips so you both have an equal chance to win," I said.

The brothers nodded, and Matthew began flipping his silver dollar. He'd completed five flips when we heard two cops and Daniel making their way down the basement steps.

Within minutes, the cops had untied me, handcuffed the Wilson twins and led them up the basement stairs to their squad car. Matthew, Daniel and I were told to stay put until a pair of detectives showed up to take our statements.

"Guys, I can't wait any longer in this damp, smelly basement," Matthew said. "I think I'm going to faint from those gasoline fumes."

Daniel and I grabbed Matthew by his arms and led him from the basement and onto the front lawn.

As we waited for the detectives, Matthew turned and asked me, "How'd you manage to get the Wilson twins to buy into your plan?"

"I didn't think they would at first, but the more I thought about how dumb they'd been in dumping Pearson's body at your Halloween party instead of leaving it here, the more I figured they'd like my plan for getting rid of us."

"It was brilliant, and it definitely gave me enough time to text Daniel and have him bring the cops," Matthew said, patting his partner's arm. "But, there's one thing I still don't understand. Why wasn't Pearson wearing a Donald Trump mask?"

"Who knows?" I replied. "The Wilson twins probably idolized Richard Nixon when they were growing up, and the mask may have been a keepsake they owned. Besides, they needed something to cover Pearson's face after they whacked him and brought him to your Halloween bash. Now, if those detectives would get here, I might be able to take an afternoon nap after all.

MY TRIBUTE TO SUZANNE HARDING

One day in 2003, my co-worker, Matt Keating, told me about a new mystery bookstore that had opened in Carmel and how this woman wanted to start a critique group there. Since Matt and I were both interested in writing fiction, we visited the store and that's where we first met Suzanne Harding.

Suzanne was the perfect person to lead our critique group. She had accumulated a wealth of life experiences working as a cab driver, secretary, art director, college photography instructor and a chef. And, her Catholic education in Indianapolis and elsewhere had given her a solid foundation in writing and thinking logically.

If you wanted to be a writer, Suzanne believed, you needed to write. She insisted on everyone in the critique group handing in a writing sample every two weeks. For some, this assignment became too burdensome, and our ranks dwindled. But for those of us who remained, we soon learned the fictional techniques that it took to get our short stories published in mystery anthologies, locally and around the country.

I was devastated in March 2018 to learn that Suzanne had passed away. She had become a less frequent part of our critique sessions because of the demands of publishing a romantic thriller each year. Our critique sessions were never the same without her.

Thank you, Suzanne, for all that you did to help us become better writers. We miss you dearly and dedicate this *Circle City Crime* anthology in your honor.

D. B. Reddick

LOST AND FOUND
SHARI HELD

"Where the hell am I?" Liz asked herself as she awoke in an unfamiliar bedroom. The room looked like a bottle of Pepto Bismol had exploded—pink-flowered wallpaper, pink-polka-dotted white area rug and a frilly, pink-and-white checked quilt on the scroll-patterned brass bed. Unless they'd redone the rooms to host a Mary Kay convention, there was no way this was the J.W. Marriott in downtown Indianapolis.

A tap on the door startled Liz from continuing her observations. An elderly woman bearing a covered tray entered. "Maria, I'm so happy you're awake at last," she said, beaming in Liz's direction as she gingerly placed the tray on the polished mahogany nightstand next to the bed. "It's so nice to meet Eric's soon-to-be bride. Eric's my favorite nephew, you know."

Liz sat up straight at that. "But, I'm not—"

The old woman sat on the bed beside her without missing a beat. "I'm Sylvie Thayer, but you can call me Aunt Sylvie. Eric told me all about your little D&D problem—drinking and drugs. D&D. I thought up that little jewel myself, Maria. Kind of catchy, don't you think? Anyway, don't you worry, dear. I'm good at keeping secrets—especially family ones. I'll take real good care of you until Eric arrives."

Liz opened her mouth but Sylvie stuck a spoon in it before Liz could protest. "Try some of this chicken noodle soup—one of my specialties. It'll make you feel better." The tray also held a small loaf of freshly baked bread and a generous slice of some kind of pie.

Liz ducked and dodged the next spoonful even though the savory aroma made her mouth water. "First of all, I'm not Maria. I'm Liz Le Clerc, an acquisitions editor for Partridge House Publishing. Secondly, I don't have a "D&D" problem. Thirdly, and more to the point, where am I, how the hell did I get here, and where's my god-damned luggage, purse, and friggin' cell phone?"

Sylvie raised her hand, palm facing Liz. "Now, no need for such colorful language, dear. Eric won't like that one bit once you're married. Bad for the ears of all the beautiful little offspring you'll have. It's just the alcohol talking. I smelled it on your breath earlier." She moved closer to Liz and touched her punk-purple hair. "Oh, my. We'll have to do something about this before the wedding."

Liz smacked Sylvie's hand away. "Look lady, I'm not Maria. And there isn't going to be a wedding—at least not with me as the bride. Now, tell me where I am and how I got here."

Sylvie sighed. "You must be having one of those brownouts I read about when researching your little problem. Well, here's what I know. You're in Indianapolis. I assume you drove here from St. Louis. Eric told me to be on the lookout for you. Anyway, I found you sacked out in a lounge chair when I went outside to water the flowers. I figured I must not have heard the doorbell, and you'd fallen asleep while waiting for me. You looked pretty out of it, so I brought you inside to lie down while I hustled up a light lunch."

Liz digested that information. *What the hell?* She was missing something—something like…she looked at the clock on the nightstand…close to two hours. "Do us both a favor and call me a cab! I'll figure it all out at the hotel."

"That's just the alcohol speaking, Maria. No cab. No hotel. Until you own up to being Maria, you're staying right here."

Sylvie raised up with an agility that surprised Liz and sprinted toward the door. Before Liz could catch up to her, Sylvie slammed the door and turned the key.

# # #

And it just keeps getting better. Liz ran her hand through her hair and sank back down on the bed. Indianapolis was the last stop on her two-week, whirlwind acquisition tour. She was here to size up Jon Moore, an eccentric breakthrough writer her publishing house was interested in signing. She remembered leaving her bag at the carousel and speed-walking through the airport in search of the bar.

That's the point where her memory got kind of crunchy. She vaguely remembered talking to a man who offered to give her a lift to the hotel. The next thing she knew, she was here. Looney-tunes land.

The whole scenario would have been comedic—except for the part where she'd lost two hours. And for the part where she was now being held prisoner. It felt like she'd been dropped into a chapter of Stephen King's *Misery*.

Maybe she should be more concerned, but Sylvie didn't worry her. Liz was in her early thirties, athletic, and model slim. She could take out the pint-sized blue-hair with one well-placed karate kick. Not that she saw any reason to get violent. At least not yet. Liz spread some butter on a piece of crusty bread and popped it in her mouth. Sylvie was one weird lady, but her food was to die for.

The meal momentarily distracted her from the full fury of a pounding headache. She hadn't felt this miserable since last year's office party where some joker had spiked the "punch" with a deadly concoction of eleven different liquors.

Liz took a deep breath and struggled to make sense of her plight. Headache or no, the big mystery she had to solve was how in the hell she had ended up at Sylvie's house. And why couldn't she remember what had happened between the airport and here? The only thing that made sense was that she'd hit her head or she'd been roofied. She felt for bumps or cuts but found nothing.

Okay. Roofied it is. Either that or I'm missing my marbles and I truly am Maria from St. Louis. She shuddered at the thought.

But first, she had to figure out a way to escape. Sylvie Thayer might be harmless, but Liz certainly wasn't going to stick around to meet Eric. She needed a plan. Life was always better when you had a plan. Her best bet was to pretend to be Maria…

# # #

Liz pounded on the door to attract Sylvie's attention.

"Hold your horses, young lady, I'm coming!" Sylvie unlocked the door. "I suppose you need to use the facilities. The bathroom is down the hall and to the right."

"Thank you, Aunt Sylvie," Liz said, giving her best shot at sounding contrite.

Sylvie's face softened and she beamed at what she must have considered a term of endearment.

If she's really a sweet old lady I'm going straight to Hell for this.

"But what I really need to use is your phone. I promised to contact a cousin once I got here and let him know I arrived safely."

"Certainly, Maria. Family is very important. But are you sure you're up to it? I mean, you seem lucid enough now, but…"

"I'm feeling much better. I think I just needed a little food in my stomach."

"My chicken soup's good, and some say it can cure the common cold in two days flat, but just to be safe, I'll call Doc Daniels and have him check you out after you get through talking with your cousin. The phone's this way."

"Okay. Sylvie, what's your address? I want to let my cousin

know in case he can drop by."

"You're in Speedway—home of the Indianapolis 500—at 802 Winner's Row." Sylvie sat in a rocker and took up her knitting.

Liz silently thanked her stars for her ability to remember phone numbers and dialed Jon's cell phone. He didn't pick up. She'd have to leave a cryptic message.

"Hi, Jon. This is Maria—your cousin from St. Louis. I know we were supposed to meet up at the J.W. Marriott at seven o'clock this evening, but my plans have unexpectedly changed. I'm now staying in Speedway with Sylvie Thayer at 802 Winner's Row. Long story. Speaking of stories, how did you like the movie version of Stephen King's *Misery*? I now know firsthand how James Caan felt. I hope to see you—" Beep.

Suddenly Liz felt as drained of energy as a scarecrow that had lost its straw stuffing. She barely heard Sylvie making her call.

"You look white as Mrs. Murphy's albino cat. Why don't you lie down until Doc Daniels gets here, dear?" Sylvie helped Liz to her feet and walked her down the hall.

Liz lay on the bed but her mind wouldn't let her rest. It was ludicrous, but what if this were an elaborate charade Jon Moore had created to impress her? If that were the case, the good news was she wasn't in any danger; the bad news was he'd probably fall out of his chair laughing at her call for help.

That scenario wasn't likely, but it also wasn't unprecedented. Once, a wannabee Montana author showed up for their meeting in the guise of his main character, a gun-toting, whiskey-drinking cowboy. It was hysterical until he got carried away and accidentally pulled the trigger, shooting himself in the foot. Then there was the F. Scott Fitzgerald clone attired in a silk smoking jacket. He offered her hallucinogenic absinthe while discussing his upcoming book between puffs on a pretentious cigarette holder. Plus, there were the letters offering her a week's use of Hyannis Port beach houses or ultra-modern San Francisco penthouses with views of the Golden Gate Bridge. Like it was possible to bribe her to recommend a book for publication. Liz snorted at the thought.

She understood the motivation, though. It was a tough world for unpubs, newbies, and second-tier writers. Their chances of launching a James Patterson-like writing career were about as good as winning the lottery. But if this Indy author had fabricated an elaborate ruse to stand out from the crowd, it had just backfired. Big-time. Liz wasn't in the mood.

She slid out of bed, wincing as a sharp pain made her head spin. She jiggled the doorknob, but as she suspected, the door was once again locked.

# # #

A dusty RAM pickup parked under the shade of a mature elm tree in Speedway.

The lone occupant pulled out his iPhone and selected a number from his Favorites.

"Suzanne, it's Jon. I'm at Sylvie's house. I don't see anything suspicious, but Liz's message sure sounded like a distress call. Claiming to be someone called Maria and referencing *Misery*—this just doesn't add up. And she's not answering her cell phone."

"That is strange," Suzanne said. "How could she have found out about Sylvie, I wonder? Did you drop Sylvie's name anywhere in the pitch for *Lost Girls* you sent Liz?"

"Nope. I always protect my sources. That's one of the first rules you hammered into our class."

"Hmm. And why in the world would Liz think she was in danger from Sylvie? I admit I'm stymied, too. Better stay there and observe. Let me know if anything happens."

"Um, just did. Doc Daniels showed up, and guess whose driveway he pulled into? I wonder what that's all about."

"Curious and curiouser. Hang on. I'll be there as fast as my old hips will let me."

# # #

"Doc, I'm so glad you're here," Sylvie said, taking his hand and leading him inside. "As I said on the phone, my nephew's fiancée is acting peculiar. Initially she said she'd lost her short-term memory. Kept saying she was somebody else. And the language."

Sylvie rolled her eyes and shook her head. "Eric told me she hits the booze and pills too much and too often, but this is...well, to use a phrase I wouldn't normally repeat, it's freaking me out. Right before I called you, she appeared to remember her name—Maria—but then she just wilted and obviously started feeling bad again. I'd feel so much better if you examined her."

Doc Daniels smiled. "I'd be happy to look at her, Sylvie."

"She's in here," Sylvie said, turning to unlock the first door off the hallway as if it were perfectly normal for her to have someone locked inside. "Maria, this is Doc Daniels. He's going to examine you to make sure you're okay." Sylvie looked at the doctor. "I'll be in the kitchen if you need me."

Liz sized up the doctor. He was a young-ish, golden-haired hunk. Professionally dressed. She hoped he wasn't a dingbat like Sylvie. All she could do was lay it on the line with him and see what he said. "I don't know what Sylvie told you. I may have lost my recent memory, but not my mind. There's no way I'm Maria, her nephew's fiancée!"

"I'm sure you're not," he said, looking strangely relieved. "You have to excuse Sylvie. Her granddaughter, Kara, disappeared a couple months ago. A pretty little thing. Only fourteen. Sylvie cared for her since the girl's mother died five years ago. The police suspect Kara was the victim of a sex trafficking ring. Sylvie's behavior has been rather erratic since then. For the record, I don't normally make house calls. But Sylvie's been through something no one should have to live through. That's why I try to accommodate her. Here, let me do a quick exam. What is your name, by the way?"

Liz automatically held out her hand. "Liz. Liz Le Clerc."

Then, the horror of what he had said sunk in and she shook her head. "That's awful about Sylvie's granddaughter. I can't imagine."

She paused a moment before plunging ahead. "Look, here's the deal, Doc. Unless you can find any signs of head trauma, I think I was roofied at the airport. The last thing I remember is agreeing to let some man—I can't remember much about him—give me a lift to my hotel."

"That's pretty risky behavior for a young woman, even if she is a New Yorker."

Liz ignored his comment and pushed ahead. "Then, voila! I show up here without my luggage or purse and no recall of the past hour or two. Does that sound compatible with being roofied? And, if that's the case, when will my memory return?"

Doc Daniels didn't respond immediately. Instead, he took his stethoscope and a few other items from his not-so-little black bag and checked her vital signs, reflexes, and head.

"No visible signs of trauma. Everything checks out okay. Do you suspect any sexual assault?"

"No, I wasn't…um, no signs at all. I've just lost a chunk of my memory. Is there a test to tell if a person's been roofied? Should I go to the hospital? Call the police?"

Doc Daniels closed his bag, then took Liz's hand and held it between both of his.

God, these Midwesterners are awfully touchy feely. Liz pulled back, and he dropped her hand.

"There are tests, but I'm not sure you want to go that route. I'm not aware of any local hospitals that have screens for Rohypnol, ketamine, or GHB—some commonly used drugs. A few labs do follicle testing, but it takes several weeks and may cost you thousands of dollars out-of-pocket. Besides, the results aren't anywhere near 100 percent accurate."

Liz frowned. She didn't like the sound of some pervert getting off Scot free. But it appeared she couldn't do a damn thing about it. Not without any memory or evidence.

"Seriously, since there's only one small segment of time you can't access, it's fairly safe to assume it will come back to you over the next few weeks or months."

"So, I guess contacting the police would be—"

"Do you really want to put yourself through all that grief for what likely will never amount to a conviction? I mean, it happened at the airport. That guy's probably long gone by now. It's your life that would be turned upside down." He raised his eyebrows and looked Liz straight in the eyes. "But if you want to involve the police, I'll be happy to make the call for you."

Liz rubbed at the faint frown lines between her eyes that had started showing up recently. She still had a whopper of a headache. She'd thought seeing the doc would make her feel better. Instead, she felt sad for all the young women who were preyed upon by sickos and angry that she could have ended up as one of them.

"Since you put it that way, I guess I'll consider myself lucky and get on with my life. *If* you can convince Sylvie to let me out of here."

Doc Daniels laughed. "No problem. I'll talk to her now. Just give me a few minutes alone with her before you join us. No need to embarrass the poor woman any more than necessary."

"Duly noted. I'll be out shortly."

While she was waiting, Liz mentally organized the rest of her day. She'd start with a call to the airport to see if they had her luggage and purse, followed by a call to the hotel. If necessary, she'd contact her office and ask her assistant to cancel her company credit card and wire cash. Soon she'd be free of the crazy lady and back on track with her life.

When Liz walked into the living room several minutes later, Sylvie looked like a schoolgirl who'd been scolded for skipping class. "I'm so sorry, young lady, er, Liz," Sylvie said. "I honestly thought you were Maria. I was trying to do that tough love stuff to help you…er, her, get sober for the wedding. I'm so sorry."

Thanks, but no thanks, you crazy Shiksa. "Look, what's done is done. I'm out of here as soon as I call the hotel to confirm my room's still available." Liz strode toward the phone.

"Hotel! No way you're going to a hotel, young lady. You're staying right here. It's the least I can do after all the trouble I put you through."

"Thank you, but I'm not sure that would be a good idea. I have to conduct a business meeting, and I'd tie up your phone—"

"You can have your meeting here. I'll provide the snacks for that and all your meals. Everything homemade. I can guarantee you won't get home-cooked food at the hotel. I've heard they buy frozen and microwave it." Her speech took on a more subdued tone. "Besides, I kind of miss having someone to cook for. It would do my heart good."

"Sylvie's a fantastic cook," Doc Daniels said. "I can vouch for that. And it wouldn't hurt to have someone looking out for you."

God, she's laying it on thick. And he's not helping. But he does have a point. And I'm so sick of hotel rooms and hotel food I could vomit. "Well, since you put it that way. It would be more convenient."

Sylvie beamed like Liz was the one doing her a favor. *Whatever!*

"How long will you be staying in Indy, Liz?" Doc Daniels asked.

"My flight's scheduled to leave tomorrow morning at eight."

"I'm due at the airport about that time. I'll pick you up around six." Before Liz could respond, he put on his hat and grabbed his bag. "See you tomorrow."

"I'll start cooking," Sylvie said. "Got a reputation to protect. You can sit at the desk and make your calls. Paper and pens are in the top drawer. Help yourself. If you need anything, just shout." She started for the kitchen, then turned and faced Liz. "Any food allergies?"

"Not that I'm aware of."

"Good! With all we've been through I'd hate to kill you with a peanut butter cookie!"

After Sylvie left, Liz crossed her fingers and made her first call. She couldn't believe her luck. United had her luggage. The representative said they'd deliver it later that afternoon. She struck out with her purse and cell phone. But one strategically censored call to her office—they didn't need to know all the details, after all—and Liz was back in business.

# # #

Across the street, Suzanne approached the truck from the rear and slipped into the cab, being careful not to slam the door.

"No need for stealth," Jon said. "Doc just left. Sylvie must be in the house alone with Liz. Have you had any inspiring thoughts on your way over?"

"Nada."

"Think we should crash the party? Or call for backup?"

"I think it's—"

The strains of Freddie Mercury's "We Are the Champions" blasting from Jon's cell phone interrupted her.

"Get that. Meanwhile, I'll be using my 'little grey cells' to come up with a plausible strategy for getting into that house."

"Jon, it's Liz."

Jon pantomimed for Suzanne to be quiet, put his cell phone on speaker, and cranked up the volume.

"Hey, Liz, where are you? Are you all right? I got your message and you sounded—"

"Yeah, about that. Don't worry. I had some problems at the airport and that situation was compounded by a case of mistaken identity. But I'll be fine. I'm staying at Sylvie Thayer's house like I said."

"So, are we still on for this evening at the Marriott?"

"Actually, I'm free now, so we can meet here as soon as you can make it."

"Super. I happen to be in the neighborhood. I can be there in, say, five minutes. The only thing is, I have someone with me. Actually, she's my writing mentor. Mind if she tags along?"

"No problem. Talking with her might give me more insight into your journey as a writer. That would be perfect!"

Jon turned toward Suzanne. "Well, this ought to be interesting. She's gone from James Caan to Mary Poppins. Something's not right. Any suggestions on how to get to the bottom of this mystery?"

Suzanne rewarded that remark with her famous stink-eye. "You've always been a pantser, writing by the seat of your pants, never knowing where you're going until you get there. Let's see how well you can wing this, Jonny Boy. But remember, there's much more at stake here than just putting words on paper."

# # #

Liz opened the door and invited the duo in. The tall, well-muscled man wore a faded denim shirt, tight Levis, Frye boots, and Ray-Bans. He didn't resemble any of the men she'd pass on the streets of the Big Apple, but the same self-possessed assurance emanated from him. His companion, a no-nonsense, gray-haired pixie of a woman, walked with a cane she wielded like a weapon.

"Jon Moore," he said, extending his hand. "And this is Suzanne Harding. Otherwise known as the person who kicks my ass to get the best out of me. At least that's what she tells me. I've often suspected she just enjoys it."

Jon smiled and dodged Suzanne's cane which was heading straight for his ankles.

Suzanne held her hand out to Liz. "It's a pleasure to meet you, Liz. I hope you have the good sense to sign Jon—he's one of the good ones. Has the potential to be great if he applies himself."

"So how did you end up here instead of the hotel?" Jon asked Liz once they were seated in the living area.

"Good question. I met someone in the airport bar who offered to give me a lift to my hotel. Next thing I knew, I woke up in Sylvie's bedroom feeling like I had a giant cotton ball for a head.

She mistook me for her nephew's alcoholic fiancé, Maria. And it played out from there."

"So that's why…Are you sure you're okay?" Jon asked.

"I'm fine now, although I may have been roofied," Liz said, nodding toward Sylvie who had joined them. "Sylvie called Doc Daniels to come and look at me. I'm lucky. If I were roofied, I was only out of it for a short time. I escaped before anything happened."

"Nice to meet you, Suzanne, and to see you again, Jon," Sylvie said.

"You two know each other?" Liz asked.

"After Kara went missing, Jon interviewed me for a story he was writing on sex trafficking." She patted his arm. "He was one of the nicer ones."

"Once again, I'm so sorry about your granddaughter, ma'am," Jon said, turning to Sylvie. "I'm dedicating my next book, the one focused on sex trafficking, to your granddaughter and all the lost girls like her. Not that it will get her back. But it might draw more attention to the problem."

Sylvie's eyes misted over. "Thank you, Jon," she said, patting the sides of her apron. "I'll go get refreshments. No working on an empty stomach allowed in this house!"

"So, Liz, do you remember anything about the man you think may have roofied you?" Jon asked to get the conversation rolling again.

"No, not at all. I've lost a couple hours. Doc Daniels said I'd eventually remember, but it might take a while."

"It was probably a crime of opportunity," Suzanne said. "After all, you were at an airport—a stranger to the city—en route to a hotel. No one would immediately notice you were missing. What do you remember about the guy you met at the airport bar?"

"Not much. Everything's kind of a blur."

"Would you mind if I asked you a few questions? I might be

able to help."

This meeting isn't exactly going the way I'd planned. I'm the one who should be asking the questions. Liz frowned.

Before she could refuse, Jon piped up. "That's a great idea! Suzanne's unequaled when it comes to asking penetrating questions. She can draw out information you weren't aware you had. The police often use her in their investigations. She might jog your memory and give us—and the police, if it comes to that—something to work with. What do you say?"

Sylvie futzed with a tray and four cups and saucers, a coffeepot, and a plate of cookies before setting them at one end of the coffee table. "I'd say, go for it. It might give you some relief and help others. Not that it's my decision, mind you."

Liz held up her hands in surrender. "All right. You win. As long as this doesn't take all day. We've got to discuss your book, Jon. After all, that's why I'm here." Liz sat straighter in her chair and took a sip of coffee.

"Don't worry. I won't let you leave Indy before we take care of business. I rather regret, however, not meeting at the hotel. Not that this isn't great," he quickly added as though he didn't wish to offend Sylvie. "But I'd have enjoyed being wined and dined by a beautiful woman—especially if my friends saw us."

Liz laughed at that. "That's classic juvenile, don't you think?"

"Just being honest."

"Hmm," Suzanne said. "Honest, but juvenile. Good thing you don't write like you act." She moved slowly and deliberately until she positioned herself between them. "Let's get on with it, shall we?" She folded her hands in her lap and leaned toward Liz, staring at her like she was absorbing her very essence.

"When was the first time you remember seeing the man you had a drink with at the bar? Was he on your plane?"

"I'm not sure if he was on my plane, but I assumed he had just disembarked. I remember thinking he was a fellow traveler when he first spoke to me."

Suzanne jotted a few words on a notepad she pulled from her large, Navaho-patterned tote bag. "And when was that? Where were you when he asked if you'd have a drink with him?"

Liz frowned and bit her lip. "I, I don't think he asked me if I wanted to have a drink." She drummed her fingers on the table. "I think I was headed in that direction. I might have asked him where the bar was."

"So, he followed you. Do you always frequent bars so early in the day?"

Liz felt the blood rushing to her face at that. "I'd just finished editing a book on the plane and all I had to look forward to was yet another dreary, soulless hotel room. Let's leave it at that, shall we?"

"Okay," Suzanne said. "You've said you can't remember anything about the man. But, since you travel often, what kind of man, in general, would you have a drink with in an airport bar? I assume he would have to be within a certain age range, maybe dress a certain way? Don't try to remember the actual person. What we're going for here is a general profile that he might fit."

"Sure. Well, he wouldn't be scruffy. He'd probably be well-dressed."

Jon snorted. "Guess that leaves me out, huh?"

Both Liz and Suzanne glared at him.

"Okay, call me a snob, but he would likely be a businessman, perhaps wearing a suit. No wedding ring. Well-groomed. Able to talk in complete sentences with subject/verb agreement. Not someone wearing earbuds and totally attached to his iPhone." Liz was warming up to this. "Extra points if he carried a book."

"Good job, Liz. That's more information than we had before. Now, what do you remember about the bar itself? Were you sitting in a booth or on stools? What did you order?"

"I'm sure I ordered my airport standard—a Tanqueray and tonic on the rocks with a lime twist. It's safe. I've only been to a few places that managed to screw up a gin and tonic. We were sitting at a table with high stools. I remember, because I'm so short. That stool was a bitch…" Liz stopped in mid-sentence. "I, I had to step up to get into his vehicle. It was an SUV of some sort."

Jon groaned. "Only about one out of every three vehicles in Indy are SUVs."

Suzanne shot him a look that would have stopped a herd of buffalo in its tracks.

"Good," Suzanne said. "Your memory is returning. You're beginning to recall actual things about that time. What about the color or make of the SUV?"

"Hey, I'm from New York, remember? I wouldn't know a Ford from a Cadillac." Her eyes opened wide. "But I recognize the Mercedes-Benz trademark. It was a Mercedes."

"Now, we're getting somewhere. Go back to when you first stepped into the car."

Liz nodded.

"What else did you notice? What kind of music was playing on the radio? Did you see any distinctive items?"

"It was classical music. Beethoven, Bach—one of those guys. I remember him phoning someone and telling them he had one more stop to make and then he'd be over with the goods. The goods! That was me the son-of-a-bitch was talking about, right?"

Jon stretched his arm across the table and put his hand over hers. "It's all right. You got away from him. You're safe now."

Liz swallowed hard. Sylvie scurried over and offered her some water, which Liz gratefully took.

"Now, I know this will be hard, but place yourself back inside the car. What do you see, smell, feel?"

"The tan leather seats were cushy. And they were a perfect match for his gloves."

Sylvie's cup crashed to the hardwood floor and shattered. "Doc Daniels." Sylvie's voice was so quiet they all strained to hear what she said. "Doc Daniels drives a Mercedes with tan seats that match his gloves." She looked at Liz. "And he was right here in the neighborhood when you appeared on my deck. You must have escaped from his car while he was here seeing me. I was the stop he had to make."

"Now, Liz," Suzanne said, taking her hand. "Close your eyes, let your mind go blank, and return to the car. Can you remember anything about the driver?"

"No. But I remember a black bag on the floor of the back seat. You're right, Sylvie. It was him. It was Doc Daniels. When he came to check up on me, he mentioned something about my being from New York. I hadn't told him that—at least not here. Not at your house. Did you tell him I was from New York?"

"No. You never said where you were from—just that it wasn't St. Louis."

"There's no way he could have known unless I told him that at the airport."

"Or from the I.D. in your purse," Jon added.

"We've got him," Suzanne said.

"But he was here, and he treated me. How could I not have remembered it was him?"

"You were drugged," Jon said. "That messes with your mind." He turned to Suzanne. "Time to bring in our buddies at the IMPD. They should have enough to act on."

Liz turned white as the linen blouse she was wearing. "Doc Daniels…He, he was going to take me to the airport tomorrow morning."

Jon looked like he could kill. "That son-of-a-bitch! He was going to get you in his car and finish the job, then. You would never have made it to the airport."

They were all silent while they digested that information.

"Do you think he had anything to do with Kara's disappearance?" Sylvie asked, her eyes as grim as death itself.

"I don't know, but if he did, we'll soon find out," Jon said.

# # #

Several days later Liz sat in the office of the IMPD officer in charge of the case. While simple and functional, the room wasn't exactly bare bones like she'd expected. The floor was manufactured wood, instead of linoleum and the chairs were worn, but comfy. His bookcase held photos of a pretty, middle-aged woman, Liz presumed to be his wife, and a daughter whose life was chronicled from birth to high-school graduation.

"We found your purse and iPhone in the doctor's SUV," he said. "That backed up your statement and gave us what we needed to arrest him. Fortunately, he's cooperating with us."

"So, why'd he do it? He had everything going for him—good looks, good career. I don't get it. What caused him, a doctor, to do such an awful thing?"

"Turns out the good doctor had a weakness for gambling. He wasn't particularly good at it and he'd racked up thousands of dollars in debt at the local casino. Unfortunately for him, the casino's owned by mobsters. Sex trafficking is one of their sidelines. They agreed to let him live if he'd abduct young, good-looking girls and women for them."

"What a jerk! Didn't he care how many lives he destroyed? So much for the Hippocratic Oath."

"He was the perfect grabman. The operation had previously lost several women to accidental overdoses during abductions. Not only did Doc Daniels have access to drugs and the knowledge to correctly administer them, he was attractive and above suspicion. Kara Thayer didn't think twice about getting into the car with her grandmother's doctor." He shook his head.

"But why Kara? Someone he knew. Wasn't that risky?"

"He needed to get his quota or face the consequences. We've known about the casino's sex trafficking connection for years but haven't been able to prove it. The doc's a slime bag, but he's the lynchpin that will help us bring down the entire sex trafficking ring—at least locally.

"He tried to relieve his guilt by taking good care of Sylvie. Based on his statement we, along with our FBI partners, rescued ten other girls before they were shipped out and sold to the highest bidders."

"Any word about Kara?"

The sergeant shook his head. "We're working on some leads, but nothing solid yet. You can bet we'll follow up on anything we get our hands on."

"At least Sylvie has some hope."

The phone on the sergeant's desk rang. He glanced at the read-out, then looked up at Liz. "I've got to take this. You take care."

"Sure thing. Thank you, Sergeant."

He swiveled his chair so he was facing the other way and started talking on the phone as Liz let herself out.

# # #

Four weeks later Liz got off the plane at Indianapolis International Airport and took a cab straight to the J. W. Marriott.

Thirty minutes. I've got to hustle if I'm going to beat him there. She peeled off her traveling outfit—a black tunic paired with black tights—and changed into a pale-pink girly dress that set off her purple hair. Technically, as Jon's acquisition editor, she was here on business. From a purely personal perspective, she'd kind of like to see where this mutual attraction thing might go. She touched up her Nars Orgasm lipstick, then hurried out the door.

Liz beamed as Jon entered the dining room at Ruth's Chris. He looked a little out of his element wearing a suit and tie. But she'd been insistent. It's not every day a relative book virgin signs a three-book contract with a top-notch publisher. Partridge House had already received a few nibbles for movie rights for his sex-trafficking thriller, *Lost Girls*.

"You look fantastic," Liz said. "I could get used to seeing you in a tie!"

"Better take a snapshot, because the next time you see me like this will be—"

"Oh, here's our champagne," Liz interrupted. "You did say you missed being wined and dined. I think this qualifies. And we've got a lot to celebrate!"

"Not all of it having to do with the book deal, I hope," Jon said, handing her a flute of bubbly champagne. "Well, business first. Here's to Lost Girls."

Liz just smiled. "And here's to you for finding one more of them. Me. Cheers!"

MY MEMORY OF SUZANNE HARDING

I met Suzanne when Michael Eldridge and I attended a writing seminar sponsored by the Indianapolis Public Library. She was on a panel discussion with Terence Faherty. Something she said sparked Michael's attention, and after the seminar he asked her a few questions. She asked him what he wrote and other questions and then invited him to join *In Mysterious Company*, the critique group she had founded years ago. He nodded in my direction and said, "My wife also writes. She writes chick lit." Suzanne looked at me like he had said I served people poison mushrooms for breakfast. Then she added, "Well, she can come too." So, that was my entry to the group.

Suzanne gamely read through my chick-lit submissions, saying, "You're a very good writer. But, why don't you try writing mysteries?" I opted to go the hybrid route, writing chick-lit mysteries. When I got stuck in the middle of a book, she urged me to try my hand at writing short stories. While I still prefer writing novels, I've had two short stories published in other anthologies. So, I guess she had a point there.

I wanted my story in this anthology to be about writing and authors to honor Suzanne. In *Lost and Found*, she's a mentor like she was to many people in her lifetime. This story also raises awareness about crimes against women and children which is a cause I'm sure she would find worthy.

This one's for you, Suzanne. RIP.

Shari Held

MARIBETH, THE TROPHY WIFE
MB DABNEY

"911. What's the nature of your emergency?"

"It's my husband. I just found him when I got home. On the floor," replied Maribeth "Mare" Hutton. "He's been shot."

Detective Drake Curtis listened to the recording of the 911 call several times, paying close attention to the caller's tone and calmness. Given the victim's high profile in the community, Drake noted that some people on social media were taking a harsh view of the victim's young widow, with many calling her a black widow—one of the kinder expressions.

Having been assigned the case, it was up to Drake and his partner, Morgan Barrie, to discover the truth.

He was still familiarizing himself with all the facts in the Hutton case when Barrie walked into the squad room. She placed a small white bag on Drake's desk.

"I stopped at Long's Donuts on the way in," Barrie said.

"Thanks," Drake said, reaching into the bag and pulling out a donut with chocolate sprinkles. He took a bite and washed it down with some coffee from the office pot. He grimaced slightly.

No amount of cream or sugar could improve the taste of the

coffee in the office.

Drake and Barrie shared desks that faced each other, and she took her seat. "So how's the case lookin'?" Barrie said, dunking a glazed yeast donut into her coffee, which was a light tan color.

"It's not looking good," said police Capt. Marcia Wood as she strode up. She eyed the bag of donuts in silence before turning her full attention to the officers. Though generally not known for such hesitation, she took a breath before she addressed them.

"This Hutton case…the public is clamoring. The press, the TV stations. It's all over social media. Rumors everywhere. I got the chief and the mayor all over my ass. Everyone wants answers," Wood said. "Find some and find them quick."

# # #

In the hierarchy of wealth, there's new money and there's old money. The difference is discernible, even to the less well-heeled. It's the difference between The Rock and a Rockefeller.

New money is first generation wealth, whereas old money is passed down for generations. New money tends toward a flashier show of wealth—in the purchase of expensive houses, cars, jewelry, clothes, and even women. Old money tends toward classic designs—in the maintenance of houses, cars, jewelry, clothes, and even women.

Maynard Hutton, president and CEO of the Indianapolis Wildcats, was a contradiction—a combination of the new and the old.

Hustlin' Hut, as he was called in school and later in the pros, was born poor on a farm outside of Nashville, Indiana, in rural Brown County. Named a Mr. Basketball during his senior year of high school, he played power forward at Indiana University. But he was too small for that position in the NBA, so when the Indianapolis Wildcats drafted him in the second round, they moved him to small forward.

Hutton had an impressive, though far from an earth-shattering, pro career for seventeen seasons with the 'Cats, then in New York, and in the final two years of his playing career, with the Wildcats again.

Retired, Hustlin' Hut took a front office position, where his IU management degree, along with his business acumen and savvy instincts, came in handy as he moved up steadily in the 'Cats organization.

The pay was excellent, which provided him with new wealth, as witnessed by his expensive, tailor-made suits and shirts, silver cufflinks and the Porsche 911 Turbo he drove. But his digs on North Meridian Street, by all appearances, was old money.

That, undoubtedly, was due to the influence of his wife—now his widow.

# # #

Wispy cirrus clouds floated by in a lazy, unpretentious way so as not to offend the wealthy. The sun was warm but not too much, so as not to scourge the perfectly manicured lawn of the Hutton home, a massive and carefully maintained old structure of red brick. Soft yellow daffodils welcomed Drake and Barrie on the path as they walked the last few yards from the driveway to the front door.

Drake could not hear the doorbell chime from the outside but in only moments the door opened. The officers introduced themselves to a quiet female servant dressed in pale gray and were welcomed into the front foyer. Almost immediately, an impeccably dressed man in a conservative, dark gray suit appeared from a room near the back of the house. His facial expression was that of a man who rarely comprehended a joke. He was trim, though probably from genetics, not exercise, and slightly tanned, though probably from a tanning bed and not from the sun.

Reaching the officers, Drake noted that he wore more fragrance than any man should.

"How may I help you, officers?" the man said without the least bit of sincerity.

"We are Detectives Curtis and Barrie from the IMPD," Drake said as both officers showed their identification, "And we'd like a word with Mrs. Hutton."

"I'm so sorry but it's not possible to see Mrs. Hutton at this time. She is in mourning and isn't seeing anyone," the man said in a dismissive way.

"This is an important police investigation into Mr. Hutton's death and…" Detective Barrie started.

"I understand, but…" the man said before Drake interrupted him.

"Who might you be?" Drake asked.

The impertinent question stopped the man cold for several heartbeats. "I'm Patrick Cook, Mrs. Hutton's personal attorney," he said as if announcing he was the queen's equerry.

"We could do this downtown," said the six-foot-two Drake, taking a step forward and looking down at least six inches to Cook, who took a half a step backwards.

But in a flash of theatrics and false bravado, Cook reached into the breast pocket of his jacket and pulled out a cell phone. "I could get the mayor and the chief of police on the line in an instant."

"That won't be necessary, Patrick," said a soft voice from above and behind Cook. With her hand on the polished wood banister, an attractive woman in her late thirties slowly descended the stairs from the second floor.

Thick carpeting muffled Maribeth Hutton's steps as she glided down the stairs. She wore a simple, knee-length, black dress—more contoured than fitted—a strand of white pearls and black pumps. Her blond hair was pulled back into a bun. By all outward appearances, she was in mourning. But even in grief, she was unwilling to throw her sense of fashion out the window.

The black made her appear older than she was, Drake thought, but she still was nearly two decades younger than her late husband.

"Ma'am, I am Detective Drake Curtis and this is Detective Morgan Barrie," Drake started, having mentally dismissed the attorney. "We're sorry to disturb you, at such a difficult time, but we have some follow-up questions."

"It will only take a few minutes of your time," Barrie interjected.

"I thought Mrs. Hutton answered all the questions of the first officers," Cook hesitated, clearing his throat and looking up at his client with an uncertain expression, "on the day Mr. Hutton was killed."

"Just a follow up. A formality, really," Drake said in a reasonable tone to Maribeth, instead of her attorney. "You understand, of course."

She apparently wasn't having it. "I am very busy right now…with the plans for the memorial and all. I don't have the time for this," Maribeth said with a certain firmness.

Drake did not back down.

"This is a criminal probe into a homicide, Ma'am," he said, matching her firmness. "I could just take you downtown for questioning."

"This will take less time," Barrie said, in a calmer, more reassuring tone.

Maribeth waved her hand as if it were a white flag, then turned, leading them down a hallway to a well-appointed study that was flooded with natural light from the outside. She indicated two chairs with a small table between them. "Please have a seat and ask your questions," she said with forced civility.

Maribeth took a seat on a brightly colored couch facing the officers. Cook perched himself at the other end of the couch.

"We'll only take up a few minutes of your time," Barrie said, again.

Maribeth sat with her legs crossed at the ankles and hands placed on her lap. She was as still as a granite statue—composed and stoic. Cook sat on the edge of his seat.

She nodded for them to start.

Drake knew the facts. But he loved this part of the investigative process—finding details and clues in unspoken words and gestures. The widow Hutton may not have killed her husband—the jury was still out on that question—but she could definitely shed some light on the case.

It was just a matter of discerning the facts.

"Tell me what happened that day. Start from the beginning, from the time before you arrived home," Drake said.

Barrie had a pen and notebook at the ready. Drake, on the other hand, rarely took such notes in an interview, relying on a photographic memory that rarely failed him at work, though it often did at home. He would jot notes later, so he sat back in the chair, arms folded across his chest, the image of casual disinterest.

Out of the corner of his eye, Drake noticed that the attorney Cook was sweating.

"I went to the hair salon earlier in the day for my usual Tuesday appointment," Maribeth said.

"What time was that?" Barrie stopped writing to ask.

"9:30." She paused as if waiting for another question, which Barrie did not immediately supply.

"Was your husband at home when you left?" Drake asked.

"Yes. He was in his study upstairs."

"That's where the body was found later, is that right?" Barrie asked, scratching notes as they went.

"Yes. Around three."

"Was he alone when you left in the morning?" Drake asked.

"It was Isabelle's day off. And my assistant, Janet Cummings, is on vacation. She's not back yet. No one was here."

Drake sat forward and interlaced his fingers, forming a church steeple. He rubbed the steeple fingers over his lips in a thoughtful manner. "In the police report you stated there did not appear to be a break-in. How do you think the assailant got in? Does anyone else have a key?"

"I have no idea. But nothing was missing as far as I could tell."

"And you checked," Barrie said.

"I looked around."

"Was your husband expecting anyone that day? Could he have let them in?"

Maribeth started to shake her head and Cook reached over to calm her. She regained composure quickly as Cook addressed the officers.

"Mrs. Hutton has already answered all these questions."

But she reassured him, instead. "It's all right, Patrick." Addressing Drake again, she said, "Go ahead, detective."

"Could Mr. Hutton have let someone in?" he asked.

"Maynard rarely answered the door himself. He always left that to our maid or sometimes to me. Or Janet. I don't know what he did when he was alone."

Drake leaned back in his chair again. Relaxed.

"What did you do after your hair appointment?" Drake asked.

"I went to the café at Nordstrom's at the Fashion Mall for tea and some lunch," she said and was stopped by Barrie's next question.

"Alone?"

"Yes, I was alone," she said and paused. "The waitress may remember me...I go there quite often...but there's no credit card receipt, if that's what you're getting at. I paid cash."

"What did you eat?" Drake asked quickly.

"Crab bisque, and an arugula salad with berries and figs," Maribeth said.

"You remember that?" Barrie asked.

"It's a good salad. I like it a lot."

"And what did you do after lunch?" he asked.

"Went shopping in the mall for a couple of hours."

"Still alone," Barrie said, stopping her note-taking to wait for the answer.

"Yes. Alone. Only window shopping. I didn't buy anything."

"No witnesses?" Barrie asked.

"No."

Drake exhaled heavily, deliberately. He once again held the attention of the room as he drummed a finger on his lips. Finally, he said, "Tell me about what happened when you arrived home. That was what time?"

"She said three o'clock," Cook said.

"Thank you, counselor, but I was asking Mrs. Hutton," Drake remarked. There was always a chance someone might slip up on a detail, so it was worth asking the same question more than once.

"I called upstairs to say I was home. It was around three."

"You do that generally when you get in? Announce yourself?" Drake asked.

"Yes, most of the time," she said. "I didn't get a response but didn't think much of it. I just assumed he didn't hear me. He might have been working."

"Did you think your husband was home at the time?" Barrie asked.

"Yes."

"Why's that?" Barrie asked.

"His car was in the garage when I came in."

"Did anything seem unusual or out of place when you arrived?" Barrie asked.

"No. Not at all."

"What happened next?" Drake asked.

"I busied myself in the kitchen for a few minutes but when I didn't hear anything from upstairs, I went up. I thought he might be taking a nap and I checked the bedroom, but he wasn't there. Then I checked his study. And there he was on the floor. He'd been shot. There was…blood."

"And that's when you called the police?" Barrie asked.

"I don't know. I think I screamed first and then called the police."

"Did you touch anything? The body? Anything at all, as far as you know?" Drake asked.

"No, I don't think so. I just called the police."

"From the study?" Barrie asked.

"Uh, yeah. I was in the study."

"So you did touch something. The telephone and probably the desk. But you just said you didn't touch anything," Drake said.

He allowed the statement to hang there, gauging her reaction, then took the interview in a different direction. "How long were you married, Mrs. Hutton?"

"I'm still married," she corrected with a firmness. "It's been about fifteen years."

Drake did not flinch at the chastisement. "When did you meet?"

Maribeth started to fidget a little. Drake made a mental note.

"It was just before I finished college at U of I…the University of Indianapolis," she said. "We met when he made a visit to campus for some sports promotion event. We hit it off almost immediately. It was right at the end of his playing career."

"Are you a big sports fan, Mrs. Hutton? Of the Wildcats?"

"No, not really. I go to the games sometimes. The big ones, of course," she said, her tone of disinterest unwavering. "I went recently to all the home games in the conference championship and all five games in the NBA finals. We won, of course, as you know. Against Memphis, four games to one. We were all happy about that. But, no, I'm not a big sports fan."

Barrie cleared her throat. It was a signal they worked out beforehand, when it was time to ask the most uncomfortable question and Barrie, as a woman, would do the asking. Barrie adjusted in the chair and looked squarely at Maribeth. She spoke in the softest tones she could muster.

"I'm so sorry to ask…"

"Then don't," Cook said and nearly rose from his perch on the edge of the couch.

Drake didn't speak but gave the attorney a stare so cold it would chill a cup of hot tea. Cook settled but he didn't relax. Maribeth, on the other hand, remained impassive.

"Like I said, I'm sorry to ask but surely you understand. It's our job," Barrie said.

Maribeth gave the briefest of nods.

"How had your relationship been recently with your late husband? Had there been any problems of late? Financial…or otherwise?" the detective probed lightly.

Drake gauged Maribeth's non-verbal response. Most people, in such a circumstance and faced with such a line of questions, would display some sort of nervousness—shifting body position, looking away if only briefly, absently scratching some part of their body. But with Mare Hutton, there was nothing but silence, a silence neither detective broke.

Until finally…

"I love Maynard and he loved me," she said with little obvious emotion. She didn't take her eyes off of Barrie.

Drake noticed that Cook appeared pleased with the answer. He, on the other hand, was not.

"Excuse me, Ma'am, but you evaded the question regarding the state of your marriage," Drake said.

Maribeth's eyes moved to focus on Drake before she slowly turned her head to face him.

"There was no problem, whatsoever. We have a wonderful marriage. Maynard was very happy," she said.

She got up, ending the interview, and the others also rose.

"If you don't mind, I'm tired. It's been a difficult time and there's still so much to do before the memorial service," she said, walking to the door of the study. She indicated the door at the front of the house. "Isabelle will show you out."

Drake spoke for both officers. "Thank you for your time, Ma'am. You have our deepest sympathies for your loss."

And with that, they took their leave.

# # #

At the end of the driveway, Drake turned the car to the right, heading back downtown. "Whatever she's hiding, it must be big," Drake said as he took one last look at the house fading in his rearview mirror. "Let's go over what we've got so far."

Barrie flipped through notes from the passenger seat. "She confirmed pretty much what she told the officers. She came home around three, found the body, shot dead on the floor. No sign of forced entry. Nothing stolen. She didn't contaminate the crime scene," Barrie said, looking up. "Hey, that vehicle ahead has an expired license plate."

Drake passed the vehicle without looking over. "Skip it. Just go on."

"They were married fifteen years. Comfortably wealthy. No large debt. Standard insurance policies and no new policies," Barrie said, again looking at the road. "Pennsylvania would be quicker than Meridian."

"Let me drive, okay. Go on."

"Maribeth Hutton has no criminal record. In fact, prior to seventeen years ago, there's no record of her at all, of any type we've been able to find," Barrie said. "Is that why we drove up there? You hoping she'd suddenly spill her guts to you on who she is and where she came from?"

"I wanted to size her up," Drake said. They drove for a few moments in silence, even as Drake nearly ran a red light at 22nd Street.

"Division of labor," Barrie said. "Since you're lead on this case, what's your pleasure?"

Drake seemed to smile to himself. "Given your love of basketball…"

"Michael Jordan could've gotten elected president back in the day," she said.

"...and your love of Chicago..."

"Southside, born and raised," Barrie interrupted again.

"I won't have you suffer the indignity of going down to the Wildcats office. After I drop you at the office, I'll follow up with the team and see if anything is happening there," Drake said.

"Her story about going to the hairdresser and the department store...I'll see if anyone can corroborate any of that," Barrie said. "And it'll give me a chance to see what's new at Nordstrom's."

Slow traffic finally forced Drake to turn left and head over to faster-moving Pennsylvania Street.

"We are going to have to dig a little deeper to find out about her past," Drake said. "I'll work on that."

"And what's your gut telling you about the lawyer?" Barrie asked with a certain merriment in her voice. "Given your hatred of lawyers and your thinly veiled contempt for Cook, it might be a good idea that I handle that part of the investigation."

"Agreed," Drake said. "And if nothing big turns up in the meantime, we can regroup back in the office later this afternoon to compare notes."

"The captain said she wanted to see you as soon as you got back," said an officer as Drake dropped his things into a drawer at his desk. Drake nodded and headed for Wood's office.

The captain's office was in the far corner of the floor. The upper half of the office had a large glass window, thus allowing those outside to see in as long as the blinds weren't drawn. When the door was closed only muffled sounds escaped the office.

The door was closed but the blinds weren't drawn when Drake walked up. Wood was sitting at her desk and an assistant police chief, whose back was to the window, was standing over her and talking forcefully. Then, he abruptly turned, flung open the door and left.

"Chief," said Drake as the man passed and only received a grunted "detective" in return. Drake looked up at Wood, who motioned him into the office.

"Have a seat, detective," she said as she walked around her desk and hiked a hip onto it. She took a deep breath. "They're hopping mad upstairs. Some lawyer called complaining about you and Detective Barrie questioning his client."

"We were only doing our job," Drake replied, but she waved it off.

"I know that. They know that," Wood said, pointing a finger upward. "That's not the problem." She planted both feet on the floor but remained leaning back on the desk. "There's all this pressure, particularly from the Wildcats, to solve the case. People are impatient. And they think everything is like it is on TV. Murders are solved in under an hour."

Wood mostly allowed Drake to do his job without undue influence on its pace. Results were always the priority, not speed. But he always kept her filled in and thus gave her as much detail as he could.

At five, Drake and Barrie hunched over their desks for the last time that day to discuss their day's findings. And an hour later, Drake headed home to his wife, Shelley, and young daughter, Dana.

Though it was not on his normal route home, he drove up Meridian, enjoying the view of the beautiful homes and immaculately well-kept lawns. As he passed the Hutton abode, he noticed a large number of cars in the drive, undoubtedly belonging to those helping the grieving widow put the final details together for the big, public memorial service planned for the next day.

Unfortunately, Drake was no closer to finding the man's killer.

# # #

Drake's wife, a pediatrician, had an overnight emergency and so it was up to him in the morning to get their daughter up and ready for summer day camp at the Y. As a result, he headed into the office a little later than normal.

And again, he took Meridian Street.

As he approached the Hutton house, something looked slightly amiss, so he turned around at the nearest corner and headed back. In the driveway near the back, virtually unseen from the street, was a car Drake had not seen on his previous trips past the house. And since there was a massive memorial service for Hutton scheduled for downtown in the basketball stadium, Drake hadn't expected anyone to be at the house.

The front door opened as he approached, and a woman came out.

"Oh, I hadn't expected you," she said, startled at the sight of the large black man on the front step. She didn't close the door behind her, perhaps as a means of escape.

"I'm Detective Drake Curtis of the IMPD," he informed her, taking out his identification. She looked at it and then up at him. She didn't seem reassured of his presence. "And you are…" he said.

"Uh, I'm Mrs. Hutton's assistant, uh, Janet…" the woman said haltingly. She looked the part of an efficient assistant, though she didn't appear as Drake might have imagined. "I was away."

Neatly dressed in conservative navy slacks and a tan blouse, she was trim, blond, in her early fifties and unusually pale, even for a white woman. Clearly, sunbathing wasn't something that interested her.

"Yes, I was told you were on vacation," Drake said.

Janet finally closed the door behind her and together they headed for the driveway.

"I'm just back. They had a hard time reaching me. I was in the South Pacific when it happened. I rushed home as soon as I could," Janet said. "Mare asked me to look after the house today during the service. To make sure no one came by."

"Prudent," he said as they reached his car.

"You don't mind, do you? I need to make a quick run to the store and then get back."

"No, that's fine. You weren't here when we stopped by before but I think I have everything here that I need," he said, sliding onto the driver's seat. She waved as he pulled out and left.

# # #

There are times when Drake can't think at his desk. No inspiration from the board where they track evidence and suspects. No inspiration from Barrie or colleagues. It's then that he knows he needs a change of venue to clear his mind and with the Hutton case staring him in the face, he concluded it was that time.

He looked up at the board.

Patrick Cook.

While it was still a stretch, a case was forming around the lawyer. He had the motive—money. The CFO at the Wildcats confirmed that the Huttons were canceling his retainer at the end of the month, and would be using the 'Cats' legal team. And Cook had opportunity because of his access to the house.

But Drake's gut told him something was amiss, and so he walked several blocks to a small coffee shop on the corner at the Circle. It provided a perfect view of the fountains at the base of the Soldiers and Sailors Monument. He settled in at a small table near the back but facing forward. Steam rose from a cup of strong black coffee as he studied a notebook for some hidden clue. He focused so intently on the case that he didn't immediately notice the step-slide, step-slide of a person approaching.

He looked up, and there was Suzanne M. Harding.

If ever there was a Yoda in the real world, it was Suzanne. She was a pixie of a woman, with short gray hair and ragged bangs on her forehead. She walked with a cane, favoring one leg, and had on what Drake considered as her uniform—a pair of jeans, a simple, high-neck top and a sweater, which was amazing considering how warm it was outside.

Just like with Yoda, Suzanne could be overlooked at first glance. But to do so was at one's own peril. She was sharp, quick-witted, possessed an inquisitive mind and had a wicked smile that displayed a row of crooked teeth that were yellowed as much from age as from the cigarettes she smoked.

Suzanne was an author of both fiction and true crime, and was blessed with instincts Drake rarely saw outside of law enforcement. She could spot clues better than most detectives.

Drake stood as she neared the table, as much out of respect for Suzanne as for a sense of chivalry.

"Suzanne," he said. "What a surprise."

"Detective Drake Curtis, mind if I join you?" she said with genuine politeness.

Drake moved halfway around the table and pulled out a chair for Suzanne to sit down. He took her cane, putting it on another chair, and she placed a folder with some papers in it on the table.

"Would you like…" he started, before she said, "Yes. A cup of hot tea."

He went for the drink and several minutes later returned to settle back in his chair. Their two cups and the folder separated them from across the table. "What are you doing here?" Drake said.

"I knew you would never accept anything for speaking to my class at The Writers Center about your investigative police work and I wanted to thank you. Therefore, I bought you this," Suzanne said, reaching into the folder, pulling out an envelope and handing it over.

He quickly opened the envelope, pulled out the card and read. The inscription brought a smile to his face. But when he looked up, Suzanne was studying him with serious intent.

"You could have mailed this," he said. "I assume it's not why you're here."

Suzanne slid the folder closer to Drake's side of the table, nearly knocking over his coffee. "There's been so much speculation in the media regarding who killed Maribeth Hutton's husband and internet trolls have been saying all sorts of really nasty things about her, calling her a gold digger, a trophy wife and a black widow. I wanted to speak up for her."

"How'd you know it was my case?" he asked.

"I didn't. But I knew you'd know whose case it is and might vouch for me," she said. "That's why I came downtown. To talk to you, or someone, about Mare. I was told in your office where I'd find you."

Suzanne stopped and then picked up the tea for a sip. Drake studied his companion across the table. Her eyes were intense and dark. And he concluded there were strong emotions ready to burst forth from her otherwise calm exterior.

He waited for her.

"No matter what the media might say, Mare Hutton didn't kill her husband," she said. "She couldn't. She's not that type of person."

"How do you know that?" he asked.

"People hate. And haters always blame a younger woman when something happens to an older man. They say, 'She did it,' no matter what 'it' is."

Drake leaned forward and placed his elbow on the table. He stroked his chin as he looked at Suzanne, then, looking down at the folder, he moved back from the table. "What's this going to tell me?"

She didn't answer the question but said, "The community here in Indianapolis is small. Very small. Intimate, and not just in a physical or sexual way."

Suzanne paused again but kept her eyes on the detective, perhaps judging whether he understood where she was going.

All Drake said was, "Go on."

"For a couple of years, Mare Hutton was seeing a good friend of mine. Helen Payne. Helen was an amazing woman. Loving, caring, passionate. She was incredible," Suzanne said as if holding back emotions that threatened to overwhelm her at any moment. Her eyes moistened. "She was a great wife and mother to two kids. She and Mare, they were so good together. But they had to keep things secret. They had too much to lose. Their families, their lives, money, security. Everything.

"Helen had taken one of my courses on female crime writers, which is how I met her and then, ultimately, how I met Mare. They would come by the house and we'd sit and drink wine and laugh and talk," she said. "They would sometimes spend the night together in my spare bedroom. They loved each other. My space was the only place where they could openly show that love without judgment or shame."

Suzanne succumbed to tears, dabbing her eyes with spare napkins. Drake waited for a minute before jumping in.

"Love is a powerful emotion, Suzanne. Some people are willing to kill because of it. You know that. Certainly if Maribeth rejected her or if Payne came to view Maribeth's husband as an obstacle to overcome, it could happen. You know it could," Drake said. He waited before adding, "Where can I find this Helen Payne?"

"Crown Hill Cemetery. She died. Eighteen months ago. Cancer. Mare was devastated," Suzanne said, finally adding, "I was devastated. She was a good friend."

"Why tell me this, Suzanne? How's it relevant?" Drake asked. Tapping the folder, "And what's this gonna tell me?"

"Mare loved Maynard. Very much. He was very caring and loving. She just wasn't in love with him. She couldn't love him in that way," Suzanne said. "But the safety and security he provided, she needed that. Because, she had a past. She didn't talk about it much...provide specifics...but I encouraged her to write about it. She did. As fiction. But I suspect some of the details, if not all the details, are true."

# # #

Suzanne left the folder with Drake in the coffee shop and he took it back to work. He was about to open the folder and read its contents when Barrie walked up.

"The lawyer, Patrick Cook," Barrie said, with a certain resigned disappointment creeping into her voice, "has an alibi for the time of the shooting. I confirmed he was at his attorney's office, working on a strategy to keep the Huttons as clients." She paused again before adding, "I guess that leaves us back at square one."

Barrie sat down at her desk facing Drake. He leaned back in his chair and looked up at the evidence board stationed to his right. They would have to cross off Cook as a person of interest. For now, that left only Maribeth.

"Hutton wasn't having any trouble with anyone associated with the team. The players, coaches, management, the staff. They all loved him," Drake said. "I haven't gotten even a hint of a mistress. The team says he was totally devoted to his wife. What about her hair dresser and Nordstrom's at the mall."

"I was able to confirm the hair appointment but nothing later. She would have had time to go home and do the deed and then go back to the mall," Barrie said.

"I've got something to read here," Drake said, opening the folder. "Maybe something will jump out at me."

# # #

The first item in the folder was a short story called "Running to Hide". And it was as remarkably well-written as the details were frightening.

Set in Massachusetts at an elite school, the protagonist was a well-to-do young woman named Mary Elizabeth Brewster, who was in her first year of college when she was orphaned after her mother's fatal automobile accident. She was left with lots of money but little else.

Vulnerable, scared and worried about her future, Mary Elizabeth found comfort and solace in the bed of her environmental engineering professor, a woman named Penelope

Nichols.

As an activist, Penelope took ever increasing and dangerous actions to advance her goal of saving Earth. She also proclaimed her undying devotion to her young lover and demanded the same in return. "I love you forever, Mary Elizabeth. Forever. I'm the only one for you and will do anything for you," the older woman said throughout the story.

In time, the reciprocation would be put to the test—and would fail.

The pair first marched and picketed, mostly around government buildings and offices. But then they moved onto more direct confrontations, such as handcuffing themselves to the front doors of companies they claimed polluted the air and water.

Finally, concluding that merely getting arrested wasn't enough, Penelope entreated Mary Elizabeth to take a more drastic step—to kidnap an executive in the paper mill company that Mary Elizabeth's family once owned.

Drawing a line, Mary Elizabeth refused. She knew the man and his family. She wouldn't have anything to do with it.

It was a fateful decision.

But it didn't stop Penelope. She and several others kidnapped the man and left him tied up and cold in the back of a car, where he froze to death as they waited for a ransom that never came.

It was Mary Elizabeth who informed on Penelope.

Arrested and tried first on federal environmental terrorism charges, Penelope went to prison, all the while proclaiming her everlasting love for Mary Elizabeth, who testified against her at the trial. Once released, Penelope promised her young lover, they would live together in peace.

Frightened by that prospect but refusing federal witness protection, Mary Elizabeth changed her name and disappeared. Authorities in Massachusetts never knew where she went.

# # #

"I've got to find out what happened back then, how much of this story is true," Drake said to Barrie after describing what he had just read.

Since it was a federal case, he decided to start with a call to the FBI field office in Boston. Within a few minutes, he was on the line with Special Agent Michael "Mikey" Flanagan, who had one of the thickest Bostonian accents Drake had ever heard.

He gave Flanagan all the details he had, hoping something would ring true. He was surprised with the result.

"I worked that case. I remember. What you've told me is almost exactly like what happened, except that it wasn't just a mother who died in a crash. Both parents died and under questionable circumstances," Flanagan said. "But that was up to local authorities to investigate and they apparently found nothing."

Mary Elizabeth was from a prominent Boston family, the FBI agent said with a certain grudging respect. "Blue bloods going back generations. Father was in banking, as I recall, but the family's money came from paper mills up in Maine."

The daughter, an only child, attended an elite women's college that bred girls for successful marriages, but she ended up getting involved with a plot to kidnap a business executive. "She told us about the plot and aided in the attempt to foil it, but it was too late. And the man died," Flanagan said.

"Was Mary Elizabeth arrested or charged with anything?" Drake asked.

"No, in large part because she helped us. But after the trial, she just disappeared. We never knew where," Flanagan said. "Now you say she's turned up out there, huh?"

"Appears so," Drake said, taking a sip of coffee and wishing he hadn't.

"That other chick…the environmental wacko…she's a piece of work," Flanagan said. "That's why the marshals are looking for her now."

"Marshals? The U.S. Marshals? They're looking for Penelope Nichols? Isn't she in federal prison?"

There was a silence on the other end of the line for several seconds, as if Flanagan was considering the implications of what he was saying.

"She was. A minimum-security facility in West Virginia. But she apparently just walked away," he said. "The thought was that she might come back up to this area. That's where the search has focused."

"When? How long ago?" Drake asked. His respiration was picking up and it had nothing to do with the coffee.

"Three, four weeks."

"What does she look like?" Drake asked.

"I'll do you one better," Flanagan said. "I'll send you the file. It has a picture."

Once he was off the phone, Drake leaned forward with his elbows on the desk and he scratched his bald head. He was trying to figure out how to proceed, but first he would wait for the FBI's case file with the picture. In the meantime, he outlined what he knew to his partner.

"I'll see how much of this stuff Maribeth Hutton's personal assistant knows," Barrie said. "She's young and real cute. Reminds me of my twenty-six-year-old niece."

Drake looked up. "What are you talking about?" he asked, puzzled.

"I went to the memorial service this morning. You knew that. And I bumped into Hutton's assistant, Janet Cummings. She'd been away on vacation. Actually, it was a honeymoon. She just got back," Barrie said. "We talked for a while before the service."

"The assistant didn't attend the service. She hung out at the house to watch over things. I met her there," Drake said, as a sinking feeling gripped his chest. "She's not in her twenties. She's a middle-aged white woman."

Ding. He got an email notification from the FBI.

"Get one of them…Maribeth or her assistant, or both of them…on the phone right now," Drake said as he opened his email. Without reading the message, he clicked on an attachment that held a picture. It showed a woman in an orange prison jumpsuit up against a wall that measured her height.

The Penelope Nichols staring back in the picture was a younger version of the woman Drake met earlier that day at the Hutton house. But it was the same person.

"No answer on either phone," Barrie said.

"How long's the memorial service been over?" Drake asked as he pushed back his chair with such force it nearly fell over. "Never mind. Let's go. We need some backup."

"Where are we going?" Barrie asked as she grabbed her gear and headed out.

"The Hutton house. I'll explain on the way."

Drake and Barrie raced up town with two accompanying patrol cars, sirens blaring. They all turned off the sirens a half mile before they reached the house but left their lights flashing as they weaved through traffic.

They pulled into the driveway behind two cars, including the one Drake had seen earlier. The other officers were right behind.

As Drake and Barrie exited their vehicle, there was the unmistakable sound of gunfire. Several shots.

The officers pulled their service weapons and crouched but continued toward the front door. Before they reached the door, it flung open and Maribeth Hutton ran out, screaming for help. Immediately behind her, Cook appeared, limping and holding the back of his right thigh. Once outside, he stumbled into the bushes by the door but continued to struggle away from the exit despite his obvious pain.

The reason for their panicked exodus appeared in the doorway next. It was Penelope Nichols…holding a gun.

Wide-eyed and somewhat crazed, she searched out Maribeth

as if not noticing the police officers with guns drawn.

"He doesn't love you, Mary Elizabeth. None of them do. They never have. Not your parents. Not your basketball player. Not him," she indicated Cook on the grass. "I'm the only one who's ever loved you."

"Put the weapon down, Ma'am. NOW," one of the officers called.

More calmly but just as urgently, Drake said, "Penelope, you don't want to do this. Drop the weapon. We want to help you."

"You don't want to help me," she snapped. "You want to send me to jail." Looking at Maribeth, who stood quivering behind Drake, she added, "I love you, Mary Elizabeth. Tell them that."

"Drop the weapon. We won't tell you again," another officer said.

"I love you forever, Mary Elizabeth. Forever," Penelope said. And in one swift motion, she brought the gun to her head and pulled the trigger.

# # #

"Here, honey, and use the blue napkins, over there in the cabinet," Shelley said to Dana as she handed her daughter the utensils. "And remember, the knife and spoon go on the right, with the blade facing inward. The napkin is on the left."

Drake helped set the table.

"How did she…the woman…ah…" Shelley started.

"Penelope Nichols," he answered.

"Yeah, Penelope Nichols. How did she know where to find Maribeth Hutton?" Shelley asked.

"Apparently, they broadcast NBA games even in women's prisons," Drake said, putting water glasses in the proper positions on the table. "The Wildcats said they get hate mail directed at the players and coaches all the time, particularly after a home loss. But they rarely get such mail against any office staff. However, since so much of management staff were shown during broadcasts and in the press during the playoffs, more people saw them. And after winning, spouses, too, appeared in pictures during celebrations."

"The crazy woman saw Maribeth Hutton on television and knew she was in Indianapolis and somehow connected to the team," Shelley said.

"That's what we believe. Can't be 100 percent sure since she's dead but it's a reasonable assumption."

"And the other guy. The lawyer who got shot," Shelley inquired.

"She only got him in the back of one leg but not for want of effort. He'll recover," Drake said. "Unfortunately."

"Let's sit down to eat," Shelley said. The room had a warm, welcoming aroma as they took their places at the dining room table, just outside the kitchen.

"Can I say grace tonight, Mommy?" Dana asked. "I want to thank God for Daddy finding that bad lady."

Drake and his wife exchanged glances. "Yes, baby," Shelley said to her daughter. "You can say the grace."

Drake reached for his wife's hand, then his daughter's. He was grateful, too.

MY TRIBUTE TO SUZANNE

Perhaps the thing I respected most about Suzanne and that I will miss most about her was her intense devotion to the craft of writing. She was passionate about writing and somewhat intolerant when she thought a good writer was being careless or lazy. She was encouraging in her praise of good writing but, with her wicked smile, she also was straight forward in her pointed criticism of careless writing.

She hated that I rarely use contractions—something that doesn't come naturally to my writing given my background in journalism—and I have a tendency to give detailed location descriptions. "You're not writing a travelogue. It's crime fiction," she'd say. (Note that I made a special effort to use contractions above.)

I may not have always taken her suggestions—even Suzanne said your writing must remain true to who you are—but I never rejected her suggestions out of hand.

In the story that accompanies this remembrance, I tried to show the person I truly saw in Suzanne M. Harding. Because, in the end, I know that my writing—my craft—is better for my having had Suzanne as a writing coach and mentor. And as I improve, it is, in part, a tribute to her.

MB Dabney

LOSERS WEEPERS
MARIANNE HALBERT

"I'm going to piss on your mum!"

Dino heard an obnoxious cackle and opened his eyes a crack to see Grady already unzipping his stained jeans.

"Not kidding," Grady warned, a drunken gleam in his eyes. His tongue flicked out from a gap in his missing front teeth. "Get out of my spot or I piss all over your mum." The redhead had already started to heft his member in his hands.

Dino closed his eyes. "Whatever." He heard more cackling, then felt someone kick the sole of his foot through his sleeping bag.

"Hey, Dino?" Maude said. "He wasn't kidding, about your mom."

Dino sat up straighter, the rays of the sunrise hitting him squarely in the eyes.

"Have you seen this?" She pointed to the ground. Grady moved to a concrete block and was laughing to himself.

Dino grunted, heaving himself off the ground, his right knee complaining.

"Grady's pisser?" Dino asked.

He stepped into his boots and walked toward Maude, letting the aches and pains work through his forty-two-year-old lower back.

Wheezer, the sandy-colored mutt that roamed the homeless camp, took a sniff of the newspaper, shook his head, and wandered away. The slamming of a garbage truck thudded and echoed across the river.

Dino looked at the newspaper, a yellow trail soaking it and forming a rivulet in the dirt. Even from this angle, he recognized the face above the fold. He snatched up the paper, handling it more delicately as he realized how fragile it was. Maude took a respectful step back.

He read the headline silently. *City Councilwoman Martina Pravi – Missing.*

"What day is it?" Dino asked without looking up.

Maude rubbed her cheek. "Um, Thursday?"

"The *date*."

"It's the fourth," said a young female voice off to his left.

Dino glanced up to see the new kid working on a bicycle. She swiped a long strand of bangs away from her forehead with the back of her wrist and looked toward him. Dino acknowledged her by nodding an emotionless thank you.

The article in the *Indianapolis Star* said she left a meeting on the first and was planning to do some neighborhood canvassing in preparation for the upcoming midterms. Her daughter reported she never came home that night and didn't show up to work at the gallery the next morning.

Dino tore the article out and gingerly tucked it in the inner pocket of his faded flannel jacket. He shoved his items into his backpack and started walking toward the river.

"Not sticking around for breakfast?" Maude asked. "The ladies of St. Augustine's will be bringing breakfast casseroles and French pastries."

He shot her a look but didn't answer.

"I'll save you some!" she shouted as he walked away.

# # #

Dino had been waiting in the downtown district office for forty minutes. He recognized some of the officers. Finally, he was told the detective was ready to see him.

He pulled out the article, unfolded it, and placed it on the blotter in the middle of the desk.

"I want to know what you're doing to find my mother."

The detective didn't move, except for his eyes. They focused a little more closely on Dino, glanced down at the photo, and looked back up again. Then he seemed to make a decision. Relaxed, he sat up straighter. Indicating the chair across from him he said, "Why don't you have a seat. Mr….?"

"Pravi. Dino Pravi."

The detective took the blotter and carefully threw the whole thing, piss-soaked article and all, in the trash. He pecked on a few buttons on his computer and the printer on an adjacent file cabinet whirred into life, chugging out a couple of pages. He grabbed a legal pad and began to take notes.

"Dino, the homeless son," he said to himself. "We were going to look for you. This makes it easier."

"Wouldn't want to lower yourself by looking under the bridge?"

The detective made eye contact with him. "I'm Detective Zapata now, but before making detective, homeless outreach was some of my favorite work. I actually miss it." The hint of a smile made Dino believe the guy meant it. "A lot of good people, down on their luck. Sometimes they just need to catch a break." He clicked the end of his pen and prepared to begin writing. "When was the last time you spoke to her?"

"Two years ago."

"Special occasion?"

Dino readjusted himself in the chair. "I'd gone to her for

money."

The detective raised his eyebrows.

Dino hated having to explain himself. He'd thought he was through with that. "I lost my business. My wife left me. The bank was foreclosing on the house. I thought if I had enough to tide me over…" He grunted and stood. He paced in the small office before pausing. "I asked her to save my home. My marriage."

"And did she?"

Dino shook his head. He couldn't keep the bitterness out of his voice. "She was a tough-love mother. Said I'd *feel* better about myself if I dug myself out of this hole. I was angry—"

"And that's when you threw the vase?"

Now it was Dino's turn to raise his eyebrows.

"We've talked to Angela. Your sister's account of that day is similar except she said it wasn't a little. You asked for eighty thousand dollars."

Dino paused slightly before answering. "It was a big house."

The detective leaned back in his chair, his hands out and palms up. "She described you yelling, your mother crying."

"Mama always had it easy. She had the money. I was going to pay her back." He didn't like how defensive he sounded with that last declaration. He fiddled with a pen holder on the desk. "I'm a prideful man. It destroyed me to even go to her to ask. I thought if I could save the house, my wife would come back."

"For better or for worse?" The two men let silence hang between them for a beat. "Do you know someone named Mitch Wells?"

"My old partner. He was the venture capitalist. I came up with the venture, he supplied the start-up funds."

"He was also your mother's campaign manager. Had the yard signs in his trunk. Was supposed to meet her at a park near Fall Creek to do some canvassing. Says she never showed."

"You don't believe him?"

"At this point, everyone's a suspect."

"Even Angela?"

"Sure, even Angela," Zapata said.

The detective grabbed the pages off the printer and handed them to Dino. It was the same article, only sans Grady's piss. He also handed Dino two business cards. "You can reach me here. And you can get a hot and a cot at this shelter."

"For the price of my soul? How many sermons do I have to attend?"

"Maybe that can be your next start-up. A secular shelter. Let me know if you think of anything else."

"I don't have a cell phone, but I want to know if you find out anything."

"I'll leave a message for you at the shelter."

###

The water beat down on him. Dino scrubbed and washed his hair. He waited in line with some even scruffier than himself, and let the barber trim his beard and hair. He selected some clean donated clothes. It had only cost him two sermons. It had been a long time since he'd worn a tie. He walked back into camp and at first, they didn't recognize him.

Dino asked the girl for one of her rehabbed bikes, offering some faux leather gloves he'd gotten at the shelter in exchange. She accepted them, cutting off the fingertips before slipping them on.

Dino cycled to Mitch's house. He leaned the bike against a tree in the front yard, and recognized Mitch's Mercedes roadster in the driveway. The clothes he was wearing didn't feel quite right—the pants too baggy, the sleeves too short. Dino smoothed his tie, walked up to the house, and rang the doorbell. He heard a small dog barking from inside, a repeated yipping. A moment later the door swung open and Mitch stood before him, holding a tiny white dog under one arm. His hair was slightly grayer, but it was him. It took a moment for recognition to dawn. Mitch began to form a smile, then a look of sadness took over his face when he must have realized why Dino was here.

"We'll be more comfortable around back." Mitch pulled the front door closed behind himself and then led Dino down the front porch steps to a stone path that led to the back patio. Dino got the impression from the way Mitch looked over his shoulder he meant it would be better if the neighbors didn't see Dino at his door, and heaven forbid he let him set foot inside the house. Was anyone else even home? The patio felt like an outdoor living room. There was a firepit which Mitch turned on with the flick of a button. He set the dog down and went to the refrigerator masquerading as an oaken barrel and pulled out two beers. He popped them both on the underside of a marble counter and offered one to Dino, who shook his head.

"Oh…right. Stupid of me." He set the one beer down and took a slug from the other. The dog jumped up into his lap and settled there. "Water or club soda?" Mitch offered. Dino shook his head.

"You know, she went looking for you," Mitch said before taking another sip of beer. "Part of Martina Pravi's great homeless outreach work." He said *great homeless outreach work* like it was a tagline. A talking point. It probably was.

Dino did know. Zapata had asked him when they'd last spoken. He hadn't asked when he'd last seen her. That had been four times in the past year.

At first, she must've thought he'd left town and gotten a fresh start. But then he was arrested for shoplifting and she found out he'd been living in a local homeless camp.

Maude said a woman had come around asking questions about him. Did anyone know him? Had anyone seen him? Of course, they'd all denied it. Said the lady was about Maude's age, but a real looker. Nice clothes. Nice jewelry. Too nice for a place like this. Dino had caught part of an interview his mother did with a local TV station when he stopped by a food bank a few months later. Advocating for the homeless had become her passion. She wasn't just looking for her son. She found him. In the young men who felt they'd disappointed their parents. In the middle-aged souls who felt they'd let down their kids. In everyone who felt they'd failed themselves.

Martina Pravi had always been a philanthropist, but before the vase-throwing incident, most of her efforts had gone toward the arts. She owned an art gallery and showcased her own photography along with up-and-comers. Now, she photographed the homeless. Dino had recognized the faces, the clothes, the locales. She enhanced the images with big swaths of pastel colors, leaving small details hidden inside broad strokes.

Dino needed answers. "Mitch—"

"Yeah, I don't know," he said. He was holding his beer in one hand, petting the dog gently with the other. "We were supposed to meet in the parking lot, going to canvass...and she never showed up. I called her a couple times, texted, and got nothing."

"You've talked to Zapata?" Dino asked.

"Told him everything I know. Which isn't much."

"Was anyone else supposed to meet you at the park?"

It felt surreal sitting there, wearing a tie that felt like it was cutting off his oxygen, discussing his missing mother with Mitch. The stones in the patio didn't look real. The flame in the firepit with its too-blue base didn't look real. Dino didn't feel real being here. He was an imposter just like all the things around him.

"Martina said Angie was supposed to meet us. Thought it would solidify her image as a mother. I called Angie to see if she was still coming, and if she was with your mom. She acted like she didn't know what I was talking about." He took another drag on the bottle. "I know you are laying off, but I've got some of the good stuff, for old times' sake." He got up, the dog jumping down and following him as he pulled a bottle of Glenlivet and two tumblers from the wet bar. "Sarah doesn't like it when I drink this stuff. She thinks it makes me too introspective." He began to pour.

Dino shook his head and waved off the Scotch. "How was the campaign going?" Mitch added a few drops of water to his drink and sat back down, barely swirling the tumbler before taking a sip.

"Well, she'd just come off the debate two nights before. Depends on who you talk to, but the more objective pundits had her edge six points closer to the margin. Said people appreciated her openness on sharing her financial records, transparency. Going from city council to state senator will be quite the coup if she can pull it off." He leaned back in the dark wicker loveseat he was in, stretching his arms out across the back. "But now…this. I know she was under a lot of pressure, but this disappearing act can't go on much longer if she wants that senate seat."

That hadn't even occurred to Dino. The dog was sniffing at his feet. "You think it's an *act*? You think she ran off?"

Mitch grinned and raised his eyebrows. "It wouldn't be the first time someone dropped off the face of society hoping to hide." He took another slow sip of his drink.

Dino stood up. Mitch stood, too. Maybe a little too quickly. A splash of the Scotch hit his shirt. "Don't rush off. I didn't mean anything by it."

"If you hear anything, contact the detective."

Mitch picked up the dog and held it to his chest. "Of course."

Dino took the path along the side of the house around to the front yard, not really surprised that Mitch stayed on the patio with his dog and his drink. It had been awkward for them both.

# # #

His heart was pounding as he rode the bike toward the studio. He was dreading this stop more than any of the others. More than the police station. More than Mitch's house. Even more than the homeless shelter. He recognized Angie's yellow jeep in the parking lot. He walked toward the building and saw Angie kneeling in a deep ledge on the other side of the plate glass window posting "cancelled" signs over the announcement for the classes their mother had been scheduled to teach. Angie's eyes met his and she didn't move for a few seconds. The look on her face said *are you fucking kidding me?* She completed her task before wiping her hands and climbing out of the window ledge.

Dino walked through the door, a little dangling bell ringing as he entered the studio. He recognized the style of some of his mother's work hanging on the walls. Angie had her back to him, searching for something in her purse, her dark hair pulled up in a large, smooth bun. "Have you heard from her?" Dino asked.

She turned halfway in her four-inch heels. "No, I haven't heard from her or I wouldn't be hanging these 'cancelled because the instructor is MIA' announcements." She completed her turn and faced him. "God, you are still such a dumbfuck."

Angie fished an e-cig from her purse.

"Well, what do you think happened?" Dino asked, exasperated.

Angie stuck the vape in the side of her mouth, tightening her red lips around it. She thumbed a button on the device and inhaled into her mouth before blowing a cloud of vapor over her shoulder. "How the hell am I supposed to know?"

"I mean, do you think she just left—"

"She wouldn't do that. She's not a coward," Angie said. Dino heard, "she's not you."

"You didn't meet them that evening, for the canvassing."

"I don't know why she would have told Mitch that. Nobody asked me to canvass that night."

"Was she having any health problems? Had she gotten any threats? Anything?"

Angie began waving her hand as though he were a gnat she could wave away.

"Come on, Ang," he said, taking a step closer to her. "I know I messed up. I know I'm the great disappointment—"

"You broke her heart!" Angie yelled, stabbing her vape at the air in his direction. Her voice was trembling in a mixture of anger and angst.

"And she didn't break mine? She could've helped me save the house, my marriage."

Scorn was in Angela's eyes. "Give me a break, Dino. Wendy didn't leave you because you lost the house. You pushed her away long before you lost the house. The way you push everyone away. With your neglect and your in*attention*."

"Don't," he said, not wanting to hear whatever else she was about to say, knowing she was just getting started and knowing it would all be true. He turned and knocked something off the table. Angie scrambled to try to catch it, but it hit the floor.

"I'm sorry," Dino said, dropping to his knees to help her pick up the pieces. He couldn't even tell what it was supposed to be, or rather what it had been. Just a broken thing he didn't recognize. Angie was fighting back tears, her breath hitching in her chest. Dino placed one hand over hers. "I'm sorry." He couldn't keep the guilt and self-loathing out of his voice. She pulled her hands away, retrieved her e-cig from the floor, and stood. Dino stood up, too. He paced and ran his hand through his hair before taking a deep breath.

"Let's stay focused on Mama."

Angie relaxed slightly and nodded her consent.

"No health problems," she said. "Nothing serious, anyway." Her lips pursed like she was testing the waters. Was it safe to keep talking to him with anything but disdain? He didn't want to interrupt. "She'd gone on a few dates. A few different guys. Again—nothing serious. As far as threats, nothing extraordinary. Williams—"

"Her opponent?"

"Right. Williams is a pretty decent guy. They disagree on policy but were cordial, even friendly. So far it's been a clean campaign."

"So, the threats?"

"Mostly replies on social media. Misogynistic. Told her exactly what they hoped would happen to her. Some just didn't want a changing of the guard. Some called her a social justice warrior."

"For her work with the homeless."

Angie took another puff of her vape. "It started there, sure." She squinted at him, examining him more closely. "She started out looking for you. After a while, I think she gave up on that idea. I shouldn't say 'gave up.' *Accepted* that it might not happen. But she got to know these people. Realized how complex the problem is. Started trying to help them access housing, vocational rehab, addictions services, whatever they needed to get back on their feet. Personally, I didn't like her going into those camps. Mitch didn't either." The look she gave him held a question.

"You asking if I think someone in a camp is responsible?"

She raised her eyebrows.

"No," Dino said. "She knew what she was doing. She knew those people."

Angie chuckled. "*Those* people."

# # #

By the time he'd gotten back to the camp, gray skies threatened rain, which meant he'd have to relocate. Wheezer was resting at Maude's feet but lifted his head and gave out a brief whine at the rumble of distant thunder. Those with tents were making sure they were secure. Those without were moving farther under the bridge. Depending on which way the wind was blowing and how heavy the downpour proved to be, he might be able to stay dry if he joined them.

He heard Grady's familiar screech. "Hey, do you know how to use one of these?"

Grady was walking toward the bicycle girl. She plucked her earbuds out of her ear and they dangled across the back of her neck. He held something out to her.

She looked it over and pushed a few buttons. "Do you have the charging cord?"

"No," Grady said defensively.

"It's not going to turn on until it's charged." She looked it over some more, her fingers tracing along some writing. "Pravi," she whispered. She looked up and Dino locked eyes with her.

Dino stomped toward her.

"Oh no you don't. Finders keepers," Grady said, grabbing the camera out of the bike girl's hands.

"It's my mom's camera—" Dino yelled.

"Finders keepers, losers weepers!" Grady said, jubilant, doing a dance and using his arms to block Dino. Dino punched him and Grady went down hard on his ass.

"Hey, losers weepers!" Grady went on, indignant, still clutching the camera. Tears were beginning to form in his eyes as his voice quivered.

The bike girl shook her head at Grady. "That's a pretty complicated piece of equipment. Probably no good to you anyway."

"But it's mine," he pouted.

She rolled her eyes. She looked at her workbench, which was just a large fallen log with mushrooms growing out of it. "How about this flashlight?" Dino knew what she meant. She was offering a trade.

Grady cradled the camera closer and shook his head *no* in a pout.

She looked around again. "Bicycle bell?" She made it ding and the sound carried across the river.

He perked up, interested, but shook his head silently. "I want those."

Her earbuds.

She stared at him and then surrendered. She stood up and held out her hand, making him the offer.

"And the bell," Grady said, seeming to sense that he had some leverage for once. She didn't react for a few seconds, but then held out the bell. He gave her the camera in exchange.

She walked up to Dino and handed him the camera. He began to open his mouth to thank her, but she was already walking away. She started to pull a tarp over her work area. The best he could do was try to help. She waved him off. "Go."

He stuffed the camera into his backpack, slung it across his back and jumped on his bike. The skies opened as he rode away. He could hear Grady's new bell dinging in the distance.

# # #

Angie accepted his collect phone call and agreed to meet him at the studio. Within minutes of his arrival, Angie sat in a chair in Martina's private office and downloaded the photos from the digital camera onto the computer while Dino stood over her shoulder. She pulled up the last images that had been taken. The date and time stamp indicated they were taken the day their mother had disappeared.

"Who's the woman in the photos?" Dino asked, pointing at the screen.

"She's a local mystery and crime writer. Suzanne Harding." Angie pulled up the woman's website and sent her an email. She brewed a pot of coffee. After a while, Dino walked across the room to refill his cup and noticed the artwork on the wall. A large canvas, a man's face, half-hidden in shadow by a tattered hoodie, his mother's distinctive pastel swaths matching the tone of the picture. Dino's chest heaved and he looked along the wall to see another image. The same man. His back mostly to the camera, he was feeding twigs into a fire in a rusted metal trash can. Dino's hand began to tremble and he set the coffee cup down for fear of spilling it. He continued to look around this room. The room where his mother spent many of her waking hours. The man somber with dry leaves swirling around him. The man caught in a rare reluctant laugh. The man sleeping, his face revealing uneasy dreams. They were all him. As seen through his mother's eyes.

Angie had been filling the printer with photo stock and printing off some of the images from the camera. She asked him to refill her coffee, and when she got no response, she turned to look at him. He could sense her looking at him but he couldn't take his eyes off of the artwork. Her gaze followed his.

"Oh. Oh Dino, no." Angie said, standing. "I shouldn't have let you in here." She took a few steps toward him but he stiffened. She walked around him to refill her coffee, trying to normalize an anything-but-normal situation. Dino couldn't bring himself to look at her. He sat down in a chair and stared at the floor, his hands balled into fists, willing himself not to start screaming or smashing things. Thirty minutes later, Angie got a response to her email. Suzanne had agreed to meet Dino the next morning where the photographs had been taken at Eagle Creek.

# # #

Dino's calves were burning as he rode to meet the woman. Until yesterday, he hadn't cycled in years, and his leg muscles were complaining at the strain. He ignored the pain and arrived at their meeting point. He saw the woman with the cane. She stood near a bench in a tranquil woodsy area. He approached. She had the same short salt-and-pepper hair. It was her.

"Thank you for agreeing to meet me. I'm looking into the disappearance of Martina Pravi."

The woman studied his face. She seemed to make a decision and sat down, resting her hands on the top of her cane.

Dino pulled a stack of photographs from his backpack and laid them on the bench. A sly smile played over the woman's lips as she recognized them.

"Did she get any of the red-tailed hawks?" Suzanne asked. She continued sifting through them, looking.

"I don't know," he said, impatient. "I think she was more interested in you. People were always her thing."

"And I was here in the middle of nowhere because people are

not my thing," she laughed. Her teeth were a little crooked, but her eyes sparkled mischievously when she laughed. He could see why Mama wanted to photograph this woman.

"These were taken the morning of the day she disappeared," he said. "You might have been the last person to see her. Did she say anything about where she was going next? What her plans were?"

The woman took in a deep breath and then exhaled slowly, turning over how she was going to reply. She studied his face again.

"We talked about hawks. About the Vernal Equinox, how each season bleeds into the next. She seemed wistful. Sad even. That everything out here seemed so real and that she'd spent too much time lately talking to fake people who surrounded themselves with fake things. She said it was time to get real. She thanked me but seemed to have made a decision about something that had been weighing on her mind. She asked if she could make me the subject of her photographs. I agreed, and she said 'good' because she would have gone ahead and taken them anyway." She smiled and there was that twinkle in her eye.

Dino thanked her and scooped up the photographs, carefully tucking them away. He'd taken a few steps when Suzanne's voice stopped him.

"Dino," she called to him. He stopped in his tracks and turned back to her. "She also talked about her son. She was telling me about him just before I took a photo of my own." She handed him a five-by-seven black and white image. His mother, right where he was now standing. She was smiling, looking at peace. "I hope you find her," Suzanne said. "I hope you find each other." She tilted her forehead slightly forward to make sure he got her meaning. It was time to get real.

# # #

He asked Grady to show him where he'd found the camera. Grady took him behind a copse of trees farther downriver. As they walked toward the spot, Dino kept turning those words over in his mind. *Fake people who surrounded themselves with fake things.* She'd begun to sour on Mitch. As they continued to walk, Dino noticed land surveyor stakes along the way. The stakes were along both sides of the river, as far as he could see.

"There," Grady said.

Dino looked at the feet sticking out from under the shrubbery. He felt nauseous and dropped to his knees.

"I didn't piss on her," Grady assured him. "She didn't need the camera anymore. She was like this when I found it."

A low wail erupted from deep within Dino and he clawed at the land surrounding him, still damp with last night's rain. Grady looked frightened and started to back away, stumbling back toward the camp. The wail coming from Dino evolved into a primal scream that echoed down the river.

"Mama!" he screamed. He crawled forward, gently pulling the brush away to reveal her face. Her eyes were open, her gaze frozen on some distant spot. He moved forward and cradled her in his arms, rocking her back and forth.

"Finally."

Dino turned his head to see Mitch standing a few yards away.

"I come out here periodically to check on my future investment," Mitch said. "I was beginning to think you'd never show up." He took a few steps, moving closer to Dino. "I tried throwing Angela under the bus but that didn't go anywhere. Then when you showed up at my door, I thought it would be easier to get you to accept a drink, get your fingerprints, maybe even get you to pass out and wake up here. But you've turned into such a prude."

Dino gently laid his mother's body back down.

"She was a bit of a prude, too. This land isn't zoned for commercial property…yet. She was the deciding vote on the city council, and we both could've made a bundle on the deal. She'd talked so much about ethics during this campaign that she'd bought into her own talking points. Said it would be a conflict of interest to vote on this and profit from it. Kept saying, 'but what about the people who already live there?' Meaning you. She fought tooth and nail to keep this deal from going through.

"She was in my way. And now that your DNA is on her, your footprints all around, I think I will contact that detective after all."

Dino heard a dog barking, and Wheezer ran up beside him. The dog lowered his head and a low rumble began in his chest.

Maude, Grady, and the bike girl were right behind.

"It's funny how sound travels downriver," Maude said, now standing next to Wheezer.

"And even more funny how good this little doohickey records." The bike girl held up a digital recorder and played back Mitch's confession.

# # #

Zapata showed up to the scene fifteen minutes later. The cops had the place roped off. Zapata explained to Dino that they'd suspected Mitch but didn't have probable cause to check his financials or his emails. Now they did.

Angie gave Dino a ride back to the camp after the funeral. They sat in her car for a few minutes, knowing how proximate they were to where their mother spent her last moments on Earth.

"She didn't change the will, you know. She left you the house."

"What about you?" he asked.

"The studio."

"Maybe I can get it zoned for a homeless shelter," Dino said. "Or sell it and purchase several." He was only half kidding. An idea was already forming on the good he could do with it. In her memory.

"Maybe you're not so lost after all," Angie said. It was the first time he'd seen her really smile since they'd reconnected. She put her hand on his knee. "Come home."

Dino saw Maude pouring coffee for Grady. Watched the bike

girl toss some scrap of food to Wheezer.

"I am home. At least for now."

He stepped out of the car and stood in place as Angie drove away. A red-tailed hawk soared above him. He almost reached for his backpack to capture the moment with his mother's camera before remembering it was in an evidence locker somewhere. On second thought, he was relieved. He didn't want to capture this moment. He just wanted to enjoy it. The hawk screeched once before disappearing downriver.

MY TRIBUTE TO SUZANNE

When I wrote my first novel (now a trunk novel) I spoke to Jim Huang, owner of an independent bookstore in Carmel, Indiana called The Mystery Company. I told him I'd written a book and didn't know what to do next. He said that a group of mystery writers met in his shop every other Wednesday. He suggested I stop by their next meeting to introduce myself.

That Wednesday was the first time I met Suzanne Harding. I learned so much from her over the next decade. Not just the technical aspects of writing, but how to be a writer. I remember her often saying, "listen to the rhythm of the language." She was always writing, reading, teaching, and lifting others up. She genuinely wanted to help elevate everyone's writing to their best potential. She cherished Mother Earth, abhorred hubris and corruption, and had an infectious laugh.

On an otherwise ordinary day in March, 2018, I had just pulled into the parking lot to do some grocery shopping when I saw the email that Suzanne had passed. As I sat alone in my car, I read it. I read it again. I knew she'd been fighting a respiratory infection, but had no idea it would take her from us.

When I first started submitting short stories for paying markets so many years ago, she wrote this to me in an email:

"You may experience a bit of a rollercoaster, you know, up and down and all around. Just try hanging on for the ride."

Will do, my friend. I miss you, but will do.

Marianne Halbert

MIDNIGHT TWINNING
B. K. HART

He could hear the voice in his head. Male, a slight British accent. The narrative was dry, very matter-of-fact. He stood by the window. The view of new condominiums built in downtown Indianapolis along the canal; no name visible. He peered across the canal into a neighbor's home. Not creepy, more voyeuristic. A young couple in their late twenties. Young compared to him. He was graying in the temples, a little paunch to the belly. He imagined himself svelte, abs more on the rock-hard side. They were not. He sat too long behind a desk, too little time walking in the park. Got knackered more often than he should.

A cone-shaped microphone was positioned toward the open window, and he stood back, concealing himself in the shadows. After a while, he picked up a pair of headphones, placed them on his head and tapped the record button. As the tween hours grew late, the moon began its lazy trek amid the stars, while her sister image stretched long and willowy down the canal. Carter Price Vincent picked up the high-powered binoculars and trained them out the window. No blinds covered the bedroom window across the canal, so he had a clear view of the room and its inhabitants.

He didn't know her name, so he called her Millicent Abrams, Millie for short. Millie clad in her bra, her brown hair cascading down the middle of her back as she paraded back and forth in front of their bed. He'd read once that Molly was one of the top twenty whitest white girl names, and he thought the name Millie was close enough. She was alternating between laughing and screaming at *him*. Carter named *him* Andre Jackson for the same reason, Andre being one of the top twenty blackest male names. Carter didn't like to stretch his brain for trivialities like names. He preferred to save his imagination for *the rest of the story*.

For months, he watched the rollercoaster ride. Tonight was a good night. Millie was in a tiff, hyped up on goofballs. Ah, she just took a swing at poor ol' Andre. And didn't he laugh and push her onto the bed? Her muffled curses were indistinguishable from a sudden burst of voice which bled over from a neighboring condominium. Carter became distracted by the voice of a man two apartments down. He watched as the guy pulled off his shirt and tossed it onto a living room chair, still speaking into the telephone held to his ear. "Red" dressed in a plain white undershirt, plain blue jeans. Just an average white guy. Red hair. Fireman. Don't stretch too far for a description. After all, Red isn't a character in this story.

Millie freed herself from her bedding and sat up looking confused and contrite.

"Baby?" she called out. "Baby?"

Andre reappeared in their bedroom doorway, bare-chested, a Colt 45 in his hand. The beer, not the gun. Andre was a nicely built black man, smooth muscled skin, tapered waist, a snail trail of hair disappearing beneath his black jockey shorts. Millie ran a hand across the bed with a pout, then fumbled with the button on her jeans. Andre moved toward her to the bed and she screeched.

"Shut it fuckin' off."

Andre froze as if struck, then shot her a look of disgust. He placed his beer on the dresser and with a casual flick of his wrist, the bedroom plunged into darkness.

Shit.

Carter listened to the thrust and rut, the moan and chaff, but he was continually shifting the crotch of his pants for comfort. He had enough material for the evening. He popped out the tape and replaced it with a new one. He might be able to use the pillow talk in some other piece of writing. Now was his best work hour. As most of the city lay its head down to sleep, he popped his knuckles at the keyboard. He was at a point in his narrative where he needed a character to kill someone or steal something. He was thinking that tonight, he might like to steal some innocence. And onto the page he went, stealthy as a knife, easing its way through the rib cage of the story, finding a tender morsel to dissect.

Old Crow was about as good and cheap as you could get without moving into rotgut, and Carter drank far too much for hooch. He topped off his third tumbler as fingers of sunlight tickled his awareness, then he wrapped up the last bloody words of his climactic scene. He wished he still smoked; it was that good. He rocked back in his chair. A little over four thousand words. Five chapters, one of which was short, but he preferred a sprinkling of short and concise, intermingled with long passages. A rough draft but a good draft. His agent would wet her panties. She found his work raw and edgy, charged with realism. He returned the legs of his chair to the floor with a jarring thud, tossed back the last swill of his Old Crow and palmed his binoculars.

He leaned into the window frame and focused across the canal. Andre's sculptured buttock and back exposed, lighter flesh curved under and around his leg, Millie's flaccid muscled calf, pink-painted toenails. Her body mostly covered by Andre and a cheap, wrinkled periwinkle bedsheet. Her hair was a tangled mess, pushed up and over her face. One bare shoulder cut up above the fray like a shark's fin. Carter adjusted the binoculars to gain better focus, close up. There appeared to be a tattoo, from this distance, a web, with a spider lurking to its side. Huh. Interesting.

"Sasha, get back here." Carter put the binoculars down and leaned forward in the window. Below, a young woman in sweats laughed as she chased after a small dog. The clickity, click of its nails as it raced across the concrete, circling around her, darting away each time she tried to make a grab for its tiny body. "Ya big goober, get back here before someone sees you." It finally flung itself into her open arms, licking at her protesting, yet still laughing, face.

He yawned. The world was coming awake. Carter was off to sleep.

# # #

"I know you," the perky voice said, her blond head bent forward as she pushed her bifocals back up her narrow nose. "I recognize you from your dust cover. You're John Sinclair Linford."

"John Stanley Linkford, but you were close. Linford must be that other famous writer guy."

"Oh, my, how embarrassing. I am so bad with names! I do know the book though. *Midnight Twinning.* I just finished it. And, it was uber creepy. I swear I felt like I was just right there with the killer the whole time I was reading. How you get inside the mind of a psychopath like that is beyond me. Takes truly creative genius, I say. My husband says it takes the mind of a dissociative personality. To a certain degree though, all writers have to be a little dissociative, don't you think? I mean, we have to kind of distance ourselves from the story we are telling."

"I'm sorry. I didn't catch your name?"

"Oh, you wouldn't know me. I've only published short stories in small anthologies and such. My name's Janelle Crowe. I'm one of the Sisters in Crime members here locally, but this is my first time at a Magna cum Murder Festival. I think there are like twenty of our chapter members here this year, and I bet half of them decided to stay at the Columbia Club even though most of us live right here in Indianapolis. What about you, Mr. Linkford? Are you staying at the club?"

"Oh, there you are John." Kathryn Kennison touched him gently on the arm, her voice smooth with a cultured edge. "I heard *Midnight Twinning* is up for a Twisted Tales Award nomination this year."

"You hear things mighty fast, Kathryn." John grinned, pleased to be culled from the herd so early in the events. Still in jeans and a casual blue sweater, he had not yet dressed for the evening festivities. Kathryn was already decked out in a sharp, cream, silk-chiffon jumpsuit, elegantly accented with a gold bangle bracelet, a matching necklace and earring set.

"Pardon me for interrupting," she said turning her attention to Janelle. "I'm Kathryn. I don't believe I recognize you. Is this your first time?"

"Why, yes it is."

"You'll have a wonderful time. We try to keep the event small and cozy so everyone gets to mingle and spend time together." She turned back to John. "As for you, young man, since we just found out about this last minute on the award nomination, I'm going to ask you to say a few words before we sit down to dinner this evening. Do you mind, darlin'?"

"Kathryn, you could pretty much ask me to drop my drawers and streak through here butt naked and I'd say yes."

"Now, I don't think we need go quite that far, John." She patted his arm as she began to turn away. "I see Reavis over there. I need to talk to him about the *Hollywood Squares* event tonight. Suzanne Harding, good to see you this year."

A woman in dark jeans, a charcoal shirt and yellow and black striped tie leaned on a cane and returned the greeting, chatting for a moment as another woman joined them. Kathryn disappeared into the crowd, and the two women were joined by a large gentleman.

His robust, annoying voice broke into the conversation. "Who do you have to kill to get a drink around here?"

"I think they have the coffee bar on two and the restaurant bar on one, but I don't think they have a reception area bar open up here until the dinner this evening," Janelle said.

"Are you kidding me? Well, we oughta complain to the management. Who's with me?"

"Or, you could just get on the elevator and ride down to one and get yourself a drink and come on back up, George," Suzanne suggested amiably.

"George is one of our 'Mister Sisters,'" Janelle said to John as a way of introduction. "Kathryn was just inviting John to speak before the dinner because of his nomination for the Twisted Tales Award."

"I'm actually one of the panel judges for that award this year," a tall, slender brunette introduced herself. "Lindsey Kristan. I work as an agent with SMH Publishing. We sponsor the award. I've personally read all the books up for review. Our judges rank them based on previously-agreed-upon criteria. It's nice to meet you, John. I've actually only met half the authors."

"Does your criteria include a smut scale for each book?" George asked. "Because if you asked me, *Midnight Twinning* should be in the running for a *Fifty Shades of Grey* award."

"Did you read it?" Janelle huffed. "There's hardly any sex in it at all."

"It's just the trashy, looking-through-someone's-bedroom-window aspect of the whole story," George protested.

"We judges tend to focus more on the originality of the storyline. The aspects of craft involved. The voice of the author. The authenticity and feel of the story. For instance, one of the nominees, I won't mention any names, but there were holes that didn't get closed in the plot. A tracking device they claimed was used at all times, but for some reason wasn't used earlier in the narrative and wasn't explained. Small holes like that are noticeable. It really should have been caught by an editor."

"In a case like that, though, is it really the writer and the story, or is that the publisher and editor?" John asked.

"Well, you don't really know, do you?" Lindsey said. "But the story still takes the hit, doesn't it?"

"I'd be interested in hearing more about your perspective, from an award reviewer's point of view. Maybe later at dinner. I need to get down to my room and see if I can get presentable if I'm going to get up in front of everyone now."

"I'd be thrilled to share some pointers."

John separated himself from the group and slipped behind a planter, many of which had been placed around the large ballroom for decoration. He extracted a handkerchief from his pants pocket and swept it across his brow. He nearly dropped a small porcelain figurine as it climbed from his pocket with the hanky. He rubbed the doll's painted surface with his thumb and slipped it back into his pants. John wanted to change for dinner, but he caught a piece of interesting conversation.

"I'd be careful around him if I were you. His scenes feel a little too firsthand and personal, if you know what I mean."

Intrigued, John paused to listen.

"I write under a pen name. He isn't going to know who I am. I'll be fine."

"I'm just saying that I don't believe John Linkford is all he presents himself to be."

"Well, whoever is?"

His eyebrows shot up. *They were talking about me*? A small thrill ran down his spine. *How exciting.* He leaned slowly around the planter and recognized the dark pants, a hand leaning on a cane, as Suzanne. He couldn't see the other woman to whom she had been speaking. He tried to peer through the foliage to get a better look then decided to make a break for his room and try to figure out who she had been speaking to later in the evening. This was going to have to wait. If only he had worn his finger recorder. Well, too late now. He could wear it this evening. John wanted to get a good seat for dinner, too. He sure as hell didn't want to sit next to that George Mason. What an asshole. *Fifty Shades of Grey* award. George wouldn't recognize an award-winning manuscript if it fell out of a gold-plated wrapper and began humping his right leg.

# # #

"If you have joined us the last few years, then you are familiar with our version of *Hollywood Squares*. We'll be playing later this evening after we take a little break," Kathryn said winding down her speech. "Pretty much at the last minute this evening, we received news that one of our very own has been nominated for a very prestigious award this year. John Stanley Linkford is a nominee for the Twisted Tales Award based entirely, I believe, on his completely devious depiction of the character, who happens to also be an author, Carter Price Vincent. I certainly hope most of you do not pull your story ideas in the same manner as this fictional author. The latest novel in the Carter Price Vincent series is *Midnight Twinning*...which I read, and recommend highly. Won't you please give John a warm welcome?"

The room broke into applause as John rose from his seat and made his way to the podium. Kathryn touched him on the arm, then stepped away and returned to her own table where the wait staff was beginning to set out the evening meal.

"Kathryn asked me to say a few words and I very humbly and graciously said...well, I said, no—I don't have anything prepared. And, as Kathryn has been hosting Magna for many years, many of you know her—does she accept no as an answer? She says, "Why that's nonsense. You're a writer. I'll give you fifteen minutes to prepare something." He paused, patted his pocket, and said, "That was five minutes ago."

The room erupted into laughter and applause.

Kathryn called out over the noise of the crowd, "I believe what he said was that he would streak butt naked through the room if I asked him to. He couldn't wait to get up on that stage."

More laughter.

John raised his hands palm out in surrender and shook his head.

"I think the most common question I get asked is 'Where does a backward Hoosier come up with a British author who sounds so authentic?' And the answer is, we're all backward. I just tell the reader he has a British accent and then write myself into the story."

More laughter.

Good, keep them entertained. Writing murder was hard; you had to keep finding new places to hide the bodies. More laughs. Human nature was an odd thing, sometimes unpredictable under pressure. He never knew how his characters were going to react when he introduced a new component into a story. Say a false love letter pushed under the apartment door, like in *Midnight Twinning*. How was poor old Vincent to know that this small push would have created such horrendous results? Would the ending have been different if Andre had come home first, instead of Millie? As writers, we just don't know which direction the narrative will take when the unexpected occurs. And, when a white woman is acquitted for killing a black boyfriend, well how could Vincent possibly know that Millie would be stabbed to death by disgruntled inmates for escaping justice? It was a dark story, yes, he agreed. We live in dark times.

His audience remained in the palm of his hand for the full fifteen minutes. Then he excused himself, claiming his meal was getting cold and he might have to stab someone if they tried to take his salad away before he returned to his table. He checked with the crowd: They gave us knives, right? Butter knives, at least? He felt very grateful for the award nomination and thanked them for the honor. More applause, then he mumbled into the mike, "Don't piss me off this weekend or you might end up in the next Carter Price Vincent novel." He clicked off his finger recorder. Save the tape unless something interesting occurs, perhaps during dinner.

"Your Carter is more like a serial killer though. Getting away with murder story after story. Don't you find that a bit incredulous and possibly disingenuous? You write him like he's innocent, but he is totally complicit in all the atrocities that take place in the novel."

There goes that blowhard George again. How did he end up across the table from me? All the seats had been claimed when John went up to speak. He returned and had to swallow George's opinion along with the pasta primavera. There should certainly be more alcohol circulating in the room.

He was recording all the conversations. So far, he hadn't needed to open his mouth once to defend himself. Each time he started, Lindsey or Janelle took up the torch. Suzanne even jumped in a few times, surprisingly. Of course, she was on the might of storytelling and craft more so than in defense of him. Still.

"But you hate the character, don't you? And a good character gets a reaction and stays true to form," Suzanne said.

"He's not much different from the Odd Thomas characters. He does bad things, and they made a series out of the Koontz books," Janelle added.

"The motive…driving factor, is really just getting a better story out of his narrative. That's all Vincent is trying to do. When things go flat in the story, he adds a little something, to shake things up. Then he just follows where that goes." John finally inserted, "It's all about adding tension, creating discourse."

"Manipulation," George stabbed a finger in John's direction.

"Fiction!" John pointed his fork back. "We make shit up; it's what we do."

"You know what's funny about that," Lindsey cut in. "There was a story not long ago about a local woman who was acquitted and then killed by the inmates. I did some research, you know, after I read *Midnight Twinning*. Had some uncanny parallels to your story."

"Life imitates art, or art imitates life. Whichever way you choose to perceive it," Janelle said.

"And, so happens. My current story is about a woman whose neighbors believed she barbequed her husband and served him at the neighborhood picnic. Turns out, I just read a similar story in the news this week. Right here in Indiana. I'm in the middle of rewrites, and I originally had her getting away with the murder. Sometimes our characters have other ideas. Turns out Carter didn't feel the story was complete in my version, so he made anonymous tips to the police incriminating the wife. Even as I clean up the story, it sometimes changes."

"And what part did Carter Price Vincent play in provoking the wife to barbeque the husband to begin with?" George antagonized.

"Ah, for that, you will have to buy the book." John smiled.

"At a discount," George countered.

"Exactly. Double the cover price, because we're *friends*."

# # #

"It used to be the crazies only came out with the full moon around here. Now it's full on bat shit twenty-four seven," an older police officer commiserated with his partner. It was nearing midnight, downtown, Monument Circle. "Apparently a few people asked the kid to turn his music down, and he pulls a knife and starts stabbing people."

"Drugs, you think?" the young Hispanic cop, his partner, asked.

"Don't know yet. Took three officers to take him down. They got him cuffed and tossed him in the back of a squad car then started checking out the injured. A few of the witnesses turned out to be here for a mystery writers' convention."

"Bet they got some mileage out of that."

And still were. John stood about five feet away, recording as many conversations as he could get close enough to pick up on his tiny finger recorder. He had a mini camera he could affix to his glasses. He would have taped some footage if he'd worn his regular glasses…alas, all he had were sunglasses. He didn't think he could get away with the sunglasses after dark, not without raising some eyebrows.

And that's when he saw her.

On the concrete wall in front of the fountain. Her lemon sundress unusually bright as it flowed around her. Soft brown chestnut colored curls caressing her face as she threw back her head in laughter. A hint of jasmine and patchouli oil drifting on the breeze. Her signature scent. Mesmerized, John moved toward her, even though he knew better. She called out, jumping down from her perch, arms flung wide as she landed on her bare feet. And he heard it, the click, click, click as toenails met pavement. John let out a low groan.

"Sasha, you get over here." And she laughed, opened her arms and bent, and the little beast leapt into them. Then, they were gone.

The sound of honking brought John back to himself, and he looked around, startled. Not a lot of traffic on the circle in October at this time of night, but he was attracting attention from the police officers still hovering near the Columbia Club. He darted across the red brick road toward the place where he last saw her. He could still smell her. Five years.

His hand rose into the space where she'd been standing and turned icy. Memory slammed into him from Casey Key, midway down the coast of Florida where he first met Myra Jane Eastlake. She said her family had run into a bit of bad luck.

She wandered along the boardwalk singing, "I will keep my

secret around you. And it won't open like the morning flower. I will keep it in my secret compartment. And it doesn't matter that I'm a fool. Oooohh, that I'm a fool." Intrigued by her lyrics, nearly as much as her enchanting looks, he stopped her to ask what song she sang. She smiled softly, "Ah, it's something I borrowed from a little girl named Bella. It's her song."

John presumed she was part of the drift trade, working at whatever grifting came her way. Until he learned about her family. Related to John Eastlake, formerly of Duma Key, Myra rolled into Florida searching for her ancestors. Only to find a tropical storm had blown in during 2006 or 2007 and destroyed her family's ancestral home. The only thing left of Duma was a shallow area off the coast of Casey Key.

She seemed nearly as lost and yet, there was the dog. Sasha. The dog went everywhere that Myra went. "Hey, little diddle. Cool cat with the fiddle. A fancy cow that croons. And the mongrel dog aft, wee oft on the port. Whilst I danced with a wish and a broom." She rolled off the casual rhymes—this one obviously tailored after "Hey, Diddle Diddle." He really didn't think she was very good. She almost got it, but sometimes, just no. Not even close.

Myra said she was persuaded, provoked, driven…obsessed with her move to Florida. Almost as if the small voice in her head was compelling her toward a journey to find not only her roots but her future. Maybe John—was her future. And, didn't he want to be that—Myra Jane's future? And, she showed him the porcelain doll. Cupped in her hand, seemingly cherished and loathed at the same time. He always found that a bit perplexing.

"I had a wiener and some sauerkraut, yes, yes, I did. I had a wiener…such a sauerkraut and I kept him in a lid."

What did that even mean?

John never asked.

As for Sasha, the dog barely tolerated John. Click, click, click.

God, how he hated that mutt. It might have been the knowing eyes, or the way it would lean against Myra's legs and shake, the low throated growl if John reached a hand toward Myra. Yet, the damn dog made an appearance in every single one of his novels. As did Myra. Not that any reader but the most astute would ever notice that the woman and her companion managed to bleed their presence between the pages of every story he wrote. After all, he had loved her, hadn't he?

That lady, Lindsey…Kristan, was that her name? She crossed at Market Street along with Suzanne Harding. They seemed to have become fast friends. John could see a faint glow around the ladies, but more so around the agent. That's right - SMH Publishing. John thought he had a card back in his room. He felt his stomach tighten. This was a much too familiar scenario. Locking onto a new character. He should have known; Carter Price Vincent was nearly done with this last novel. John Linkford, on the other hand, was on the prowl for a new story, and a new star.

His hand fumbled inside his pocket, nerves and nonchalance. The little doll looked up at him. He wished he had buried the doll with Myra. Five years without the flesh and blood, only a cold, hard china figurine in its place. John should have broken the doll like a bad artifact and buried the remains under the little dog. He thought to put the dog with Myra's body; why didn't he think to leave the doll too?

Because he couldn't, could he. Her family had fallen on bad times, and *mi casa es su casa, eh, Kemosabe?*

He should have buried it with her body instead of letting it lead him around by the nose to each new victim. The next best seller, he reminded himself. He breathed in to quell his roiling tummy. They were disappearing into the hotel. John felt the nervousness return, anxiety rooted in resistance. He just wanted to…he just needed to…

"Move over." Her voice rang, strong and solid, inside his head.

He felt the push against his mind. Indecision shoved to the

side, John forced to the periphery as she, Myra, slid effortlessly into place.

Myra fingered the little doll, and slipped it back into John's pocket. Her gaze fixed through John's eyes upon her target, and she began to follow her. Back to the hotel, back to the writers' convention, back to the place she could begin to outline her next story. She hadn't killed a publishing agent before. But wasn't now a lovely time to start?

A SUZANNE HARDING MEMORY

I can still hear her in my mind, offering up words of wisdom.

"You can't edit a blank page."

You have to start the story somewhere in time, in place, in the seat of raw feeling.

My first encounter with Suzanne Harding was through a writing class at the Indiana Writers Center. In a moment of synchronization, I enrolled in a Short Form Fiction class that Suzanne was teaching. I was unaware she was also a fellow member of Sisters in Crime. I'd been whining to a fellow 'sister' that I couldn't find a critique group that was supportive AND fit into my schedule. I had been invited to submit a story for the critique group *In Mysterious Company*, to see if my skill level was along the lines that might benefit from the group. The class where I met Suzanne occurred concurrently as I was embarking on a new writing life with this group which Suzanne had been fundamental in starting. That was in 2015.

As a member of our group, Suzanne was always pushing us to submit more. Send our work out to publications. Encouraging us to write more, and write better. "Your words have a rhythm, a pulse, a heartbeat," and Suzanne would pound her fist in her hand, or on the table, to make her point. Her unique method in communicating her thoughts and ideas, stuck with you, leaving a little piece of Suzanne behind. In many ways, she stays alive in our writing because of how she taught. At least, that is my hope.

I feel her passing most when I come to events like Magna cum Murder, where I would see her sitting on a panel. Or at the Indiana Writers Center, where I attended her classes. My short story, *Midnight Twinning,* was half born out of this writing world, a bit of fiction wrapped around some reality and memory. Suzanne passed along so many gems of wisdom, like:

"Make your characters true to their nature."

"You have to get your butt in the chair."

Midnight Twinning is a new story which showcases Suzanne in a different, heroic, imaginary light. Whereas, the short story, *The Other Woman, (La Otra Mujer)* is an old story which has been included because Suzanne believed in the story, pushing me to shop it out to magazines. I never named the character in this story; I had a reason for this and I asked Suzanne what she thought. Suzanne told me she didn't feel the character needed a name. That was something else she was really good about...sensing when a story had enough. She often stated emphatically that readers are smart. They get it.

Of all the things "Suzanne" that I miss, I miss her voice the most.

B. K. Hart

THE OTHER WOMAN
B. K. HART

I awaken in the middle of the night to strange noises: the garbage trucks coming through the neighborhood to empty the trash at midnight. It was never like that at home, in the States. Garbage trucks came in the morning. In Spain, everything is different yet the same.

Only six weeks since I died, officially. I am still insanely wealthy here, only unknown, which is fine. It's what I wanted. To be able to hide myself away, where no one knows me, where my face wouldn't be recognized. I have succeeded. But, it's only been six weeks. And, the tourist season hasn't yet started. That will be the real test. Can I still be dead when the tourists come, or will I have to be reborn, or die again?

She settled the pen on her notebook and squinted out toward the beach becoming mesmerized by, and lost in, the waves. One wave cresting, falling over another, then again. The lulling shoosh of sound. Or should it be whoosh? It sounded more like a shoosh she decided. She picked up her pen and doodled a little in the margin along the side of her journal entry. She missed her studio, the recording equipment. But, she could still write songs. She could still write. She just couldn't sing. She couldn't do anything that looked or sounded too much like the person who had died.

"HE YA CAPA BELLO. HE YA CAPA BELLO."

Six weeks and she thought she recognized some of the words but it sounded like 'hey, ya, cap a bayou.' The harsh metallic bullhorns were a bit disconcerting at times. She pushed her sunglasses up her nose, feeling the heat from the sun on her shoulders and wondering why in the world anyone would want to buy a beautiful coat now when it was obviously becoming summer any day. The man, passing her on a bicycle, called out again through the bullhorn. "I have a beautiful coat?" He was wearing long shorts and a long sleeve shirt, but he wasn't wearing a coat. She wondered if he realized the contradiction as he rode by the *Café Cavallets* De Mar. She translated. Seahorses cafe. Little things her mind would translate when it could, like *azucar* from the sugar packets.

There was a boy, Denis. He had been helpful with her Spanish, though as often, she had been helping him with English. It was a good trade. She was remembering a lot from her high school Spanish. He was ten years old. She lied and said she was forty. It's not like anyone would know anyway, right? At least, she thought she told him forty, she might have said fourteen since she tended to mix them up in Spanish. Denis lived next door to her casita with his mother. As far as she could tell, mom was single and Denis appeared to be an only child. The houses on the beach were a bit expensive but she had the money. Her life before had given her plenty of cash. It was the fame and the loss of privacy that was the problem. She never had time for herself. It was always one more thing for someone else, no privacy, no time, just lots and lots of money and so what? What's the point of having lots of cash if you can't really enjoy who you are?

She watched as a young shirtless man in plaid pajama bottoms and flip flops led his dog into the courtyard from the boardwalk. His hair was standing on end, ruffled. The overall effect was a man who had just rolled out of bed to take his dog for a potty break. The Chihuahua, now off the leash, dashed back and forth across the stone boardwalk, sniffing corners, and racing over the curb into the sandy beach looking for a nice place to squat. So very different than the United States, here, with the way people and their dogs behaved. The man had a baggie in his hand, she noticed. This made him look very American since most Spaniards did not bother to pick up their dog's excrement from the sidewalk or any place else they happened to defecate. *Calafell* was a beautiful city, but watch your step. Seriously.

Beautiful city. Everything in walking distance. The beach. The café. The *mercado*. Oh, crap, the market. The street market only came on Fridays. She looked at her watch. If she hurried, she could still make it before they rolled up the streets, or the carts or whatever you wanted to call it. She stuffed her notebook into her shoulder bag and flagged down the waiter, Ernesto, from Cuba who "speak a very good English because I been living in Orlando, Florida for thirteen years." It was impossible to not ask questions and uncover every story when she could speak only un *poco* of a common language. Besides, he knew how to double up her *café con leche, en un vaso, caliente*. Coffee with milk, in a glass, hot.

She paid her bill, left a very small tip. Europe was different. She liked Ernesto. She tipped. He had a wife and three children in Orlando. She felt guilty leaving what might be equivalent to a quarter. As she was sliding her wallet back into the zipper compartment she saw the woman again. *Mujer loca*. Crazy Woman. She couldn't help thinking it. It was the glare from her eyes. The scowl on her face. This wasn't the first time either. It was kind of freaking her out. She didn't think the crazy lady recognized *her*, and yet the woman acted like she knew her. And, hated her. She slung her bag over her shoulder and pushed her way across the plaza. *Cara loca* fading away in the crowd. She pushed the image of the face away, far, far away.

Her strappy little sandals slapped the stones on the boardwalk in steady rhythm. Her ear picked up the beat. *Sheesst, thee-tump, sheesst, thee-tump.* Sounded like a drumstick across the edge of a cymbal with a rat-a-tat thump on the drop. Her fingers made the motion on the keyboard by her sides. She was playing air with her hands, *dedos* moving in time, her mind locked in on the beat, the rhythm, trying to set in a melody. From the corner of her mind she listened to the sounds around her.

"...and then we spend the weekend at the farm with Grandpa," said the blond girl who was maybe six. Blue dress. Blue eyes. She danced around her father, prattled on in English.

She noticed because it was English. Proper English. England English.

She lost the music. She stopped, confused. Looking around, she found the market. She had crossed the distance from the beach while she had been lost in the song, and now the spice wagons were in front of her. Three large wooden wagons, covered, with baskets of herbs and spices all labeled with their cures, not their names. Herbs for insomnia, the heart, gout, luck. Yes, that's right, there's an herb mixture for luck. Each cart had approximately sixty herbs or spices and sometimes, like now, she sneezed. Four types of pepper.

She browsed the carts as always, wondering if something strange might catch her eye. A table covered with used garments, like Goodwill in an open-air market, nice coats. *He Ya Capa Bello.* She used to have a lot of nice clothes. Costumes, one might call them. Performance outfits, maybe? Really nice coats. She could replace those, if she really wanted, sometime. *No pasa nada.* No big deal. She had put aside enough money in the new name that she could buy anything she wanted, like the house on the beach. All of that had been taken care of before she "died." All her goodbyes said. They might not have known it at the time, but she did. She tried to make sure all the good ones got one last moment with her. Something special just from her.

It had been all over Facebook. The news. Entertainment Tonight. So many people who thought they knew her. Telling stories she had never heard before. It was interesting to hear who knew you when, when you never knew them at all. Interesting, and a bit sickening. A bit weird. Maybe, narcissistic from the right perspective. They showed some nice clips though, from when she was younger, a fresh face. She had forgotten about those. She had been so skinny back then. Her hair had been so big. Big, with a capital B. It had made her feel a sense of loss. She watched it happening like it was another person, disconnected, not her at all. In a way, mourning, along with the rest of the world; they for the loss of the singer they really only knew through the music; she, for the loss of self, so very long ago. The fakers and the takers. The walkers and the talkers. It would make for good song lyrics. She'd have to remember those lines; or, more likely those lines had already been used.

Some people liked the scent of the *carnecita,* but it smelled like dead animal to her. She enjoyed the *fuet* though, and it was cheap in the market. She bargained with the man in the stall while he tried to explain to her how his *fuet* was better, the best in the land, wait...the whole world. She laughed, pushed the sausage away and began to leave, waving her hands at him to go. She offered a ridiculously low price, one euro. He knew she wasn't a native, and he'd told her five for the *fuet*. Normally, you wouldn't haggle at the street market in *Calafell,* but she had seen this guy before and they both knew she was going to pay two euros but it was harmless, *divertido*—funny, a flirtation. She paid her two euros. He wrapped a piece of brown package paper around her purchase, tempting her with samples of his other wares, prolonging her departure. She thanked him, and politely said no, putting her package into her bag and moving on down the stalls.

She wove her way through the crowd of people past tents of colorful shirts and pastel dresses, row after row of assorted fruits. She plucked a strawberry and sampled its sweet juice based solely on its heady sweet smell. She fished another euro from her wallet and motioned to the lady, holding up the coin. The old woman took a small bag from under the table and shook it out in the air then began filling it with strawberries. She was lost in the chatter. She didn't understand most of it and then realized the old lady had been speaking Catalan, which relieved her because she had thought she had been doing pretty well with the language up to that point.

A shadow fell across her as the sun moved behind a cloud. The wind kicked up a notch and blew the salted coastal air over her sleeveless arms raising goose bumps. A sense of unease passed over her. She tucked her *fresas* into her bag and looked around. She wasn't a particularly nervous person, but she had the distinct feeling of being watched. She used her sunglasses as camouflage and pretended to scan the stalls down the street as if looking for other items from the market. She noticed the olive stand. She wanted some of those, too. She couldn't see anything out of place, but the hair on her nape was still on end. She selected her olives, paid, and the sense of being watched disappeared. Before long, she was sure she had imagined it altogether.

It was a short walk back to the beach, and she took her time. She had no place she needed to be. No one needed anything from her. This is what freedom felt like. She wandered down side streets and stopped to look at the apartments "for sale" in the real estate office window. Some very nice and fairly inexpensive houses were posted. Of course, she didn't need a house, but she loved to look anyway. She ducked into a beach front *mercado* to look at the tourist trinkets. Shirts with English logos which she already realized nobody knew the meaning of, like 'born on the internet' and 'retro style.' Denis had been wearing a shirt which read 'Butterfly Effect'. She asked him if he knew what it meant. He said sure but when she explained it, he gave her a blank look. She wasn't sure if it was her Spanish or the concept he wasn't quite grasping.

"You know, butterfly effect. The wind blows in Tahiti and creates a hurricane in Hawaii?" Maybe she hadn't explained it very well.

Back on the beach, she began to walk toward the marina. There was a time, long ago, that she had walked the beach with her mother. They would stop and talk, standing in the surf while her mother dug her foot under the sand and sifted up sand dollars. She had been so young then. Her mother dead nearly twenty years by now. She stood at the edge of the water, its cold touch rolling over her feet, splashing up her ankles. So long ago. She lost something important when her mother died, but in over a hundred song lyrics, she had never quite put her finger on exactly what had been buried with her mother. It was like being orphaned. Now felt very much like then. This new life. Except this time, she had orphaned herself.

Back then, she knew only the music. She drowned herself in the sounds, immersed herself into the lyrics, created a world where she could disappear behind a façade, a face, a voice—becoming something so much larger than she could have imagined. Her whole life became the song. Until the day the music died.

Now she was just being melodramatic. Nothing died but her. "They" said they had a body, that it had been cremated. She had wondered how "they" had pulled that particular stunt off. Obviously, she had her body with her. Physically, she was still among the living. It was her persona they killed off. But, why? With the media these days, all you had to do was start a rumor. She read online that it had been an overdose on pain medication, an alcoholic stupor, or a heart condition gone untreated, cancer she hadn't wanted her fans to know about. Someone even speculated that aliens had experimented on her and it had gone bad, only a corpse left behind. That might have been one of her more favorite stories.

But, no. So much less dramatic.

A runaway.

In a foreign country no less.

Again, why? Why would her publicist choose to kill her off? It seemed odd to her since she could reappear at any time. She wanted the escape. Made her plans to disappear. It never occurred to her to kill herself off. What made them choose that route? She was curious to know. Record sales had probably skyrocketed, true. But, if she reappeared, wouldn't the public think she was the person who had engineered the "death." Was that legal? There was surely an insurance payout, right? She was pretty sure there was something illegal in that. The real question was...would she be held accountable for what someone else had done? Would it matter? If she never returned, but then, had she wanted this to be a forever thing?

In the beginning, it seemed quite the natural solution.

In the beginning...

End of daylight, brilliant oranges fading into soft russets, brushed with violet dusky strokes disappearing behind the rolling waves she had started her day upon. Not really so much noise from the beach now, the people had mostly gone, only the roar of the waves. Rhythmic and soothing. The moon, crawling up its dark canvas, spilled pale cream light onto the night now crowned by brightly lit stars. Everything so clear, here. Mars standing big and red and alone.

Could she reinvent herself? Did she even want to try? She was losing a sense of self to Spain, to the anonymity, to the moon, the beat of the waves. She was losing all that was right with her inside of a small capsule of something that felt wrong only sometimes. It was okay today. It might be okay tomorrow. Eventually, though, she would need to take back her life. It couldn't be this way forever. Who would she be, if she were not herself?

Her feet made their own way home. They knew the way by

now. Her home was ensconced in a high brick surround and she jingled the keys to the private gate. Homes were typically walled and secured here. Yet, there was so little crime in this small beachfront town. The walls were not high, five or six feet, a small deterrent to crime or for privacy. She hadn't thought to ask. Her entry narrowed through a gardened area overhung with lemon trees, hibiscus, and bird of paradise and led to a small open courtyard, also surrounded by a wall. The courtyard had an in-ground pool, again very typical. She shifted her bag on her shoulder and opened the key fob for her shades. Most homes had electric aluminum blinds on all windows and doors to keep out sunlight, adding another level of privacy. The realtor told her to keep them closed any time she was away to keep neighbors from looking into her home. She had yet to see a neighbor from her backyard, so she wasn't sure how they could possibly see into her home whether the blinds were up or down.

She heard the raspy whisper from behind her.

"La otra mujer."

A soft, light brush, the barest twinge against her side. She dropped her bag and the strawberries spilled across the tiled floor. Drops of red, splashing on her painted toes, pooled near her feet as she went down on her knees. Other woman? What other woman? The knife bit into her shoulder and she cried out in pain as she flinched away. She sprawled onto the cool tile floor, smearing streaks of strawberry under her palms as she caught herself. She rolled away and curled into a ball, and another flash of blade cut into her flesh. The crazy woman bent over her grinning, eyes still glazed, still hating, murmuring those soft words at her, but she couldn't understand. The pain was overwhelming. She moved and felt the sting again, and again like relentless buzzing bees refusing to leave her alone. Strength left her body in a gushing river of blood, muscles trembling and weak.

La otra mujer. Esposo. Mi hombre. The crazy woman thought she had stolen her husband. This was wrong, she thought. *La mujer loca* believes I am some other woman.

Two parts of her, split. One still upon the floor. The other rising above it, and she. No one would even know, she thought, that she had died in Spain. Who would miss her after all? Was she not already dead?

AUTHOR BIOGRAPHIES

Diana Catt (www.dianacatt.com) has nineteen short stories in multiple genres appearing in anthologies published by Blue River Press, Red Coyote Press, Pill Hill Press, Wolfmont Press, The Four Horseman Press, Speed City Press and Level Best Books. Her collection, *Below the Line*, is available on Amazon. She is co-editor of *The Fine Art of Murder* (2016, Blue River Press) and *Homicide for the Holidays* (2018, Blue River Press). Her short story "Framed" appeared in The Best by Women in Horror anthology, *Killing It Softly 2,* (2017, Digital Fiction Publishing Corp). She is co-author of a play, *Deadbeat,* which debuted at the 2018 IndyFringe Festival. Diana is a microbiologist living southwest of Indianapolis, has a loving family, a socially awkward cat, and is a big fan of crosswords, audiobooks, and traveling.

MB Dabney is an award-winning journalist whose writing has appeared in numerous local and national publications. Born and raised in Indianapolis, Michael spent two decades as a reporter in Philadelphia, working first as a business correspondent for *Business Week* magazine, and later as a reporter for *United Press International* and the *Associated Press.* As an editor at The *Philadelphia Tribune,* the nation's oldest continuously published African-American newspaper, Michael earned national and state awards for his editorial writing. Michael has been a member of the Speed City Sisters in Crime since January of 2008. The father of two adult daughters, Michael lives in Indianapolis with his wife, Angela, and their dog, Pluto.

Michael Eldridge is a native Hoosier currently based in Indianapolis. His public life followed a traditional path—U. S. Air Force veteran, Bachelor's Degree from Indiana University, a stint in retail management and twenty-plus years as an Information technologist. His private path includes a lifelong interest in the occult, including time as a ghost writer and editor for a New Age publisher and fifteen years as a consulting astrologer and Tarot reader. This side of his experience provides the fodder for his writing projects, which often feature paranormal themes. In addition to the short story *Exigent Circumstance*, which appeared in this crime anthology, his flash fiction story *Confucius Say* was published in the Holly Lisle 2018 flash fiction anthology *It Happened in a Flash*. He continues to write flash fiction and short stories. His larger projects include a completed novel, *Bad Karma*, and an in-progress novel, *Demon Troubles*.

Shari Held is an Indianapolis-based freelance journalist. She began her professional career at the age of 16 writing a column for the *Greensburg Daily News*. She earned her bachelor's degree (double major in English and History) from Purdue and worked toward her master's degree at the Indiana University School of Journalism. More recently she narrated *Indianapolis: A Photographic Portrait* (Twin Lights Publishers, 2017), authored several For Dummies custom publications and edited a financial book, "Advice You Never Asked For...But wished you had!" Her first mystery story, "Pride and Patience," appeared in the Speed City Sisters in Crime anthology, *The Fine Art of Murder*, 2016. That was followed by "Murder Most Merry" in *Homicide for the Holidays*, 2018.

Marianne Halbert is an author from central Indiana. She loves creepy, atmospheric, unsettling horror as well as noir crime fiction. Her biggest inspirations are Shirley Jackson, Rod Serling, Daphne du Maurier, and Ray Bradbury. Much of her work has been described as "literary horror" or "quiet horror". Marianne creates imperfect characters who break your heart and make you think of them long after the page has closed. Her stories have appeared in *ThugLit, Necrotic Tissue Magazine*, and numerous other magazines and anthologies on the cutting edge of dark speculative fiction. Marianne has been on panels at AnthoCon and Necon, is a member of the Horror Writers Association and a member of Sisters in Crime. Marianne co-edited the Speed City Chapter of Sisters in Crime anthology, *Homicide for the Holidays* (Blue River Press). She's also a lawyer, mental health advocate, wife, mother of two young adult daughters, and wrangler of her family's mini-goldendoodle, Ripley. Marianne has two collections out, *Wake Up and Smell the Creepy,* and *Cold Comforts*. She is currently working on her first novel, *The Lady's Pocket*. Keep up with her at https://www.halbertfiction.com/, @HalbertFiction on Twitter and @HalbertFiction on Facebook. Wake up and smell the creepy!

Brigitte Kephart is an American Writer of humor, mystery and horror. She has been published in mystery anthologies, under the pen name B. K. Hart, with Speed City Sisters In Crime, and in horror anthologies through James Ward Kirk Publishing. Her latest book, *It's For Sale – A Suzanne Pepper Tale,* is a comedy set in the Indianapolis Real Estate market. She currently resides in Indiana.

D. B. Reddick is a short story writer with more than a dozen published stories to his credit. David also writes under the pseudonym, Joan Bruce. Reddick is a former newspaper reporter/editor and an insurance industry professional. He is currently executive director of the Morgan County Coalition of Literacy and is a United Way ReadUp volunteer tutor. Reddick and his wife, Rebecca, live in Camby, IN.

Janet Williams writes about murder and crime because she can live vicariously through the characters she creates. They can say and do things that would land her in jail or worse. She uses words to build a world where the people who plague her in this realm become the villains of an imagined universe. Janet writes from her home in Irvington, from a desk in downtown Indianapolis, or at the dining room table of her sister's house in Verona, Pennsylvania. No matter where she is, with her laptop or a notebook and pencil, she is able to leave this plane for the world of her imagination.

www.ingramcontent.com/pod-product-compliance
Lightning Source LLC
LaVergne TN
LVHW010913110826
845149LV00013B/2344
* 9 7 8 0 9 9 6 3 0 9 2 2 6 *